00661

KU-821-216

3424

The lads waved madly to the people on the
pavement and cheered as the small coach began
to pull away and chug off down the road.

'We're on our way!' shouted Jeff above the din.
'Let's go! Let's get at 'em!'

'Who?' Scott demanded.

'Bradbury first, and then the rest,' he laughed.
'Sandford are now on Tour.'

'On Tour! On Tour!' They all took up the chant
and the coach echoed to the sound as it left the
village behind on the first leg of its journey to
Waverley . . .

ROB CHILDS is a Leicestershire teacher with
many years experience of coaching and organizing
school and area representative sports teams. He
is the author of a number of previous titles for
younger readers about football and other sports,
including *The Big Match*. *Sandford on Tour* is the
second title in a series about the talented young
footballers at Sandford Primary School.

Also available by Rob Childs,
and published by Corgi Yearling Books:

SOCCER AT SANDFORD
SANDFORD ON TOUR
ALL GOALIES ARE CRAZY
SOCCER MAD

Published by Young Corgi Books:
for younger readers:

THE BIG CHANCE
THE BIG DAY
THE BIG FOOTBALL COLLECTION OMNIBUS*
THE BIG GAME
THE BIG GOAL
THE BIG KICK
THE BIG MATCH
THE BIG PRIZE
THE BIG STAR

*contains The Big Game, The Big Match and
The Big Prize.

*Watch out for lots of new Rob Childs titles,
coming soon . . .*

SANDFORD ON TOUR

Rob Childs

ILLUSTRATED BY
TIM MARWOOD

CORGI YEARLING BOOKS

SANDFORD ON TOUR
A CORGI YEARLING BOOK : 0 440 86320 1

First published in Great Britain by Blackie & Sons Ltd

PRINTING HISTORY
Blackie edition published 1983
Corgi Yearling edition published 1993
Reprinted 1994, 1995, 1996

Text copyright © 1983 by Rob Childs
Illustrations copyright © 1993 by Tim Marwood
Cover illustration by Tony Kerins

Condition of Sale
This book is sold subject to the condition that it shall not,
by way of trade or otherwise, be lent, re-sold, hired out or
otherwise circulated without the publisher's prior consent
in any form of binding or cover other than that in which
it is published and without a similar condition including
this condition being imposed on the subsequent purchaser.

Corgi Yearling Books are published by Transworld Publishers Ltd,
61–63 Uxbridge Road, Ealing, London W5 5SA,
in Australia by Transworld Publishers (Australia) Pty Ltd,
15–25 Helles Avenue, Moorebank, NSW 2170,
and in New Zealand by Transworld Publishers (NZ) Ltd,
3 William Pickering Drive, Albany, Auckland.

Printed and bound in Great Britain by
Cox & Wyman Ltd, Reading, Berkshire.

For my wife, Joy, whose
original idea inspired
the Sandford series

Contents

1   Golden Goals

'Great goal!' whooped Jeff Thompson as David's shot smacked into the net. 'That's another fifty pence worth from your dad.'

David Woodward grinned.

'Not to mention all our other sponsors.'

The two boys trotted back for the restart of the five-a-side game, part of a marathon Fives Football competition being contested on Sandford Primary School's playing field.

'Even those backing us for only a few pence a goal will be getting worried if we go on scoring at this rate,' David laughed. 'It soon adds up.'

'Sure does. Just keep banging 'em in. It's all in a good cause.'

The Good Cause, as Jeff repeatedly called it, was the raising of money to help pay for Sandford's unexpected and hastily arranged Easter soccer tour.

The school had been invited to take part in a big Sevens Tournament at Waverley,

nearly one hundred miles away, and sports teacher Mr Kenning had come up with even more exciting news for the players.

'I've managed to organize a six day trip for the whole first team squad,' he told them at a special meeting, describing it as the best possible way of rounding off their highly successful season. 'There are two full-scale friendly matches lined up, besides the Sevens, as well as other outdoor activities to enjoy when you're not playing football.'

To the astonished listeners it seemed almost too good to be true, especially when they learned that the programme included a day of rock climbing and cave exploring, deep underground, using all the proper equipment.

To their great relief, everyone's parents had given permission for them to go on the Tour, which the boys were soon writing with a capital T. It filled all their thoughts and their dreams, and now their energies too were directed towards earning extra funds to meet its cost.

Each player had collected a list of people willing to sponsor his team for every goal they scored during the afternoon, and they were doing their best to make the most of such generosity. . .

David's goal secured a 3–1 win and two points for Thompson's Terrors over Paul's Poachers, led by defender Paul Curtis. The match was the latest in the series between just three teams, each playing ten times.

The Terrors were now able to take a welcome ten minute breather, while the Poachers remained to do battle with John's Jokers. The Jokers were piling back immediately on to the small pitch behind skipper John Robinson, still eager for further action in their search for more golden goals.

Jeff's team collapsed on to the touchline to relax before facing their next two consecutive games.

'Any idea who's ahead?' came the question.

'The Jokers, I think,' Jeff answered, 'and then us. We'll have to beat them next game to stop them getting too far in front.'

As he spoke, Alan Clayton, the tall powerful Poachers forward, blasted the opening goal past first team keeper Ricky Collier.

'Good old Alan,' Jeff cheered. 'He's a real handful to have to mark.'

'He reckons one of his uncles has promised two pounds for every goal he scores himself,' David announced.

Jeff whistled. 'Wow! It's like being professionals, isn't it, playing for all this money.'

They were all absorbed in watching their rivals, apart from one boy who was lying flat out, eyes closed.

'How much are you being sponsored for, Gary?' David asked, out of interest.

There was no reply at first as Gary Clarke idly considered the question.

'Not as much as Clayton,' came back the sneer eventually. 'We can't all be millionaires, you know.'

'I wasn't comparing you with Alan,' David insisted. 'Only asking, that's all.'

Gary lapsed back into sullen silence, never one to waste words. David simply shrugged and winked across at Jeff, realizing he should have known better.

Jeff tried to soothe Gary's ruffled feathers. 'Doesn't matter, Gary, nothing meant. Every penny helps and so does every goal. We all know what you can do. Just stick a few more in to help us win this competition.'

Gary propped himself up, thought about making some other cutting comment, and then decided against it. He needed to keep Jeff's support. The captain had often defended him in the past when the rest of the team began to pick on him if he was playing badly.

He contented himself with a heavy sigh. 'I'm doing my best, you know. I am trying, even if it doesn't look like it.'

'I realize that,' Jeff replied honestly. 'We all want to see one or two of your specials.'

His 'specials' were well worth waiting for. The players knew they just had to accept Gary the way he was, despite his moods and apparent laziness. Because when he really turned it on he was a world beater, a more skilful, natural footballer than any of them. He had played a vital role towards the end of the season, but his unreliability and inconsistency had prevented him from actually starting many games. He had become Sandford's Super-Sub!

Mr Kenning signalled the end of the first period, and as the two teams changed round he surveyed the hectic scenes all over the playing field.

It was remarkable, he reflected, how the prospect of the Easter Tour had fired everybody's imagination. The children had responded tremendously and were, in fact, the main organizers of this all-action Saturday afternoon fund-raising bonanza. There were games of skill and chance going on everywhere, mostly of a sporting nature, with the Fives pitch as the centrepiece.

The children themselves had devised all the different games and were also running various stalls. These included a jumble sale of books and comics, toys and second-hand sports kit, which Mr Kenning could see had nearly sold out. Their friends, parents and relations were having a whale of a time trying their luck at kicking or throwing at targets of posts, skittles and hoops; attempting to beat-the-goalie and bowl-the-batsman-out; and even hurling wet sponges at brave volunteers, shivering but still smiling in their bathing costumes. All for the Cause!

The huge turn-out was sure to be profitable and would help to cut down the cost of the trip to each family quite considerably. The teacher realized it would soon be time too for the day's star attraction – the Prize Penalty Competition!

His thoughts were suddenly jolted back to the present, however, by the footballers' eagerness to restart the current game. The Poachers kicked off the second half but saw it swing in favour of the Jokers, thanks to two goals from Graham Ford, their beefy black striker.

Paul led his weary team from the field to let the Terrors resume the stage.

'Two successive defeats,' he groaned. 'That wrecks our chances.'

Alan Clayton disagreed. 'There's still time. We're only halfway through.'

'Aagh! No, don't say that, I feel dead already,' gasped Dale Gregson, Sandford's

little left winger, pretending to stagger around in horror.

'Stop messing about,' Paul commanded. 'Sit down and shut up for a while. I bet your tongue's more tired than your legs.'

Dale settled beside his friend, accepting the insults. 'Ah well, at least there's still the Penalty shoot-out to come. That'll give us a bit of a break.'

'That's about all you will get,' Alan cut in. 'Peter Duncan's going to take some beating.'

The Prize Penalty Competition was being sponsored by a local company at a pound per goal. They had arranged for Peter Duncan, the goalkeeper of nearby Frisborough Town Football Club, to come along and provide extra publicity for the Cause.

Living in Sandford village himself, he was a well-known personality and the boys could hardly wait to pit their skills against him. He was expected at any minute, but meanwhile the two school keepers were performing heroics.

Neither Ricky Collier nor his younger rival Robin Tainton wished to concede a lot of goals, each concerned about his own reputation, even at the expense of stopping their friends earning extra cash. Besides, they both wanted to impress Peter Duncan!

The latest game was level at 1–1, Jeff and Graham the scorers, when Gary popped up to settle it. He weaved his way past first two, then three challengers before slipping the ball cheekily inside Ricky's near post for a brilliant individual goal.

'Nice work, son, lovely skills,' came a loud voice and Gary flushed as he recognized its owner.

The others were green with envy.

'Huh! Trust Gary to choose that moment to show off,' David grumbled. 'I wish Duncan had seen one of my goals.'

Gary had to chuckle to himself. 'That's one up to me,' he gloated.

At the final whistle, the experienced goal-keeper had a friendly word of advice with Ricky about the danger of leaving a gap at his near post. The boy could have kicked himself for the rare error of judgement.

'Don't worry, though, we all get caught out occasionally by a clever forward,' he consoled Ricky, and then slapped him on

the back to cheer him up. 'I also saw you make a couple of fine saves. You've got the makings of a good keeper.'

That was praise indeed and Ricky glowed with pleasure for the rest of the day.

The Fives competition reached its interval with the Jokers still one point ahead, and everything else closed down for a while to allow people to watch the special event.

Mr Kenning introduced Peter Duncan to the crowd and, already tracksuited, he took up position in the goalmouth of the school's main pitch.

'He looks massive,' breathed Paul.

'It's impossible!' croaked John Robinson.

Now that they saw the formidable barrier that he presented, the boys' dreams of scoring with all of their five attempts crumbled. Even one success would be an achievement.

'Wish I played in goals this size every week, I might keep a few more clean sheets then!' quipped Duncan.

Twenty boys altogether awaited their turn but the first two shot weakly and nervously. The goalkeeper, though, had already decided that every boy would gain some glory, and so with a bit of help from him they did both score once.

He had not yet had to make a proper save – and nor did he against Gary Clarke. But it was not for the lack of trying.

Amid an atmosphere of hushed expectancy, Gary ambled in for his first attempt. He sent Duncan completely the wrong way, the ball spinning teasingly in the opposite corner of the net.

A great roar went up and the man's eyes twinkled. 'Oh yes, it's wonder boy again, I didn't realize. I see I shall have to be more careful.'

But his extra concentration made little difference. Twice more, clever shimmies of Gary's body at the moment of impact deceived him and he guessed wrongly each time.

He got it right with the next but could only turn the ball on to the post before it went in. As the spectators watched in amazement, Duncan's final despairing dive was well beaten by a powerful shot into the top corner, which no goalie in the land could have stopped.

Somewhat ruefully he retrieved the ball from the net and then joined in the delighted applause as Gary was mobbed.

The goalkeeper went up to shake the boy's hand. 'Congratulations, Gary, that was magnificent shooting. You beat me fair and square. I was certain nobody was going to stick all five past me today. I shan't forget you in a hurry.'

No-one did equal Gary's feat, although Dale, with great relish, scored four times, as did Jeff, Sandford's usual penalty taker. He saw the job as the captain's responsibility.

There were other twos and threes, with some well-placed shots, but these were

largely due to Duncan's sense of fun, as he didn't always try too hard to block them. But he did thrill the crowd with some superb saves, diving full length to cling on to low shots or tipping high ones over the bar.

He even saved a few luckily with his feet and when he was tricked, everyone hooted with glee. It was marvellous entertainment, especially when he allowed a red faced Robin Tainton to score at his last desperate attempt by deliberately letting the ball trickle comically through his legs.

Two presentations followed the final kick. Firstly the company's manager handed over a cheque for fifty pounds, a generous amount above the forty-six goals scored, and then Peter Duncan produced a surprise bonus. Before being submerged under a pack of autograph hunters, he called Gary forward and gave him four free tickets for the Town's next home game to reward his outstanding performance.

'But please don't tell my team-mates what you did,' he laughed, 'or I'll never live it down. They'll be wanting to sign you on!'

To add to Gary's bewilderment, he quickly found himself surrounded by lots of new friends!

2   *Last Minute Hitch*

All the fund-raising events soon swung back into action, including the second session of the Fives, with the Poachers gaining a narrow 1-0 win over the Jokers.

As time drew on, however, people began to drift away homewards, leaving the children to count the profits on their stalls and games. But many stayed to watch the climax of the competition.

Tiredness caused more mistakes to creep into the play although the standards remained high and the remaining spectators were treated to some excellent goals. One in particular from defender Scott Peters, a screamer from inside his own half, was later judged as the best of the tournament.

With just two games left the tension mounted. The Fives title was balanced between the Terrors and the Jokers, and they were so evenly matched that their last meeting ended in a 1–1 stalemate.

The goals came from David and Graham, the afternoon's two leading scorers.

The game finished dramatically as Jeff's sizzling shot clipped the top of Ricky's low crossbar.

'Had it covered,' Ricky teased his friend as he trooped off, the Jokers having completed their fixtures and still leading by one point. 'I'm cheering for the Poachers now. If they beat you in the next match, then it means we've won.'

'Don't count on it,' Jeff retorted. 'We won't slip up against them.'

At this stage, goals for points were more important than goals for money, and two early ones from the Poachers rocked the Terrors back on to their heels. It was only through Jeff's urging and fighting spirit that his team clawed their way back into the game and produced a real thriller.

Jeff himself, leading by example as always, reduced the arrears before half-time. His team-mates responded in the second period by first equalising through David and then going ahead at last when Gary was sent clear to score.

The Jokers stood helplessly on the side-lines and could hardly bear to watch.

'C'mon, one last effort,' John pleaded. 'There's still time.'

There was – just! Inside the final minute, Dale received the ball in space out on the left, feinted to return the pass and then cut inside, creating a vital extra second for himself. Skilfully avoiding a desperate lunging tackle, he managed to tuck the ball beyond Robin's reach from a metre outside the keeper's area.

Three goals each and a point apiece, which left the Terrors and the Jokers sharing top place with twelve points and the Poachers trailing with six.

Mr Kenning congratulated them all as they jostled happily together around the results table to check on their team's total goal tally.

'A fair result, and it couldn't have finished closer if we'd written the script for it,' he declared. 'Over sixty goals scored altogether, which I'm sure will do wonders for our Tour fund!'

As the cheering died down, he laughed and said, 'Well done. Now off you go and start to collect all that hard-earned cash from your sponsors!'

During the following week at school, the sponsorship money came in steadily to add to the amazing amount already banked from Saturday's activities.

Only Gary, almost inevitably, seemed to need reminding about collecting it and he kept finding various excuses for its non-appearance. It came as no surprise to the teacher in the end when the boy admitted that he had lost the form with all the names on, and could not remember who they were.

Mr Kenning sighed. 'Have you actually called on anybody yet?'

Gary looked sheepish.

'Well?'

'A couple of people.'

'At least that's something, and it all counts. Time's running short so that will have to do now, I'm afraid.'

'It wasn't my fault,' Gary murmured. 'Only you said not to collect money from anybody without showing them the signed form and me mam must have thrown it away.'

'Look, it doesn't matter now. Just bring in what you have tomorrow, and please don't forget.'

The boy made no reply, still looking bothered, but he returned dutifully the next day with a single one-pound coin.

'OK, Gary, thank you,' Mr Kenning said. 'Let's hope you have a good Tour.'

Gary seemed almost on the verge of tears.

'What's the matter?'

'The Tour,' he whimpered. 'I don't know if I can go on it.'

'Of course you can. It's already been agreed.'

'It's me mam. She's started grumbling about the cost and now she's changing her mind.'

Mr Kenning became more concerned. He knew that Mrs Clarke had no interest in Gary's football, and also that without a father the family were not very well off.

'It sounds like you'll have to be on your best behaviour at home to keep in your mother's good books. I'm sure it will work out all right.'

He wished he felt as confident as he tried to sound.

With all the money accounted for, including a grant from the Frisborough Schools' Football Association, it was announced to everyone's delight that their efforts had been even more successful than they dared to hope. They had managed to raise nearly half the total cost of the Tour, and by doing so had saved each boy's family a lot of money.

The Tour in fact was now almost upon them and full details of the programme of activities were enclosed in a letter to parents:

Tour Itinerary: 31 March – 5 April

Thursday	**a.m.**	Departure from school Friendly match v. Bradbury School
	p.m.	Arrival at Waverley Hostel Afternoon walk and evening swim
Friday	**a.m.**	Visit to Waverley Castle
	p.m.	Training and Sevens practice
Saturday		All day – Sevens Football Tournament Evening film
Sunday		All day – Hill walking and recreation
Monday	**a.m.**	Rock climbing
	p.m.	Caving
Tuesday	**p.m.**	Friendly match v. Lynfield School Return home

There were sixteen players in the party as Sandford had entered two teams in the Sevens Festival. They were led by Mr Turner, the Headmaster, and Mr Kenning. None of them had ever done any climbing or caving before, and if there were any lingering doubts about the possible dangers involved they were soon eased.

'The hostel's expert instructors will be supervising us,' Mr Kenning explained and then smiled. 'They'll be showing us the ropes – literally!'

The details were also posted on the sports noticeboard where a group of boys could usually be found discussing their hopes and plans for the Tour and the Tournament.

'What a Tour!' Paul enthused for the umpteenth time. 'Action-packed all the way.'

'The best bit is leaving on the Thursday morning,' chuckled Dale. 'The others have still got two days of school before they break up for Easter.'

'What are Bradbury like, do you reckon? Any good?' his friend wondered.

'No idea. We never play them normally 'cos they're too far away. We should have sent someone to spy on them!'

'Mr Kenning did say both they and Lynfield will give us tough matches,' Ricky chipped in to remind them.

Before they could reply, Jeff came racing towards them. 'Hey, have you heard?' he gasped. 'Tanby will be there too.'

'Tanby? Where?' Dale faltered.

'At the Festival of course, stupid, where else? They've taken the place of another school who've dropped out.'

The boys from nearby Tanby School were Sandford's main soccer rivals in the Frisborough area, and they had shared some memorable duels in the league and cup over the past season.

Paul recovered from the shock first. 'Are they going on a Tour too?' he asked. 'I hope not.'

31

'No. They're only having a day trip to play in the Sevens. Wouldn't it be great if we met them again,' Jeff suggested, already savouring the prospect. 'Then we could give them a good thrashing and pack them off back home!'

But with all the preparations going so well, they were totally unprepared for the disastrous bombshell the following day. Mr Kenning received a short note from Mrs Clarke.

Gary had been banned from the Tour!

The boys were stunned when the news broke. Without Gary, the success of the Tour was in jeopardy.

Gary was too upset to be questioned in depth about what had happened and only mumbled something about money.

The teacher had no wish to become involved in a private family matter, but on this occasion he felt it necessary to try and find out what the real trouble was, and to see if he could help in any way. He believed that the experience of the trip would do Gary good.

He decided to risk a lunchtime visit to Gary's home.

'Wasn't my letter good enough for you?' Mrs Clarke snapped, annoyed to find him on her front doorstep. 'He isn't going and

that's final. He doesn't deserve to. I'm not going to waste my money on him after what he's done.'

Mr Kenning looked puzzled. 'I'm not defending Gary, Mrs Clarke. But I would like to know the reason why so that I can understand the situation better.'

She explained angrily that Gary had taken some money out of her purse without permission, and this was his punishment. 'He's not getting away with that sort of thing.'

'It wasn't a pound coin by any chance, was it?'

'Yes it was. How did you know?' she demanded suspiciously.

Suddenly it all became clear. He told her about the mix-up over the sponsorship money and offered to return it. 'It doesn't excuse him, I know, but I'm sure he meant well really. He didn't take it for himself.'

Mrs Clarke calmed down slightly but remained doubtful. 'I'll have to think about it,' she said at last, 'but I can't promise

anything. You can keep the pound, and you can have these back as well. . .'

She disappeared inside for a moment and then produced the free match tickets. 'He won't be needing these any more. He'll be too busy doing chores and errands to make up for his behaviour. Perhaps that will teach him a lesson.'

Back at school, Mr Kenning began to feel more optimistic about Gary's chances of rejoining the Tour, and called the boy into his room to explain about the tickets. Gary shrugged off their loss, and agreed it was a small price to have to pay if it helped to make amends for his lapse.

Team captain Jeff was the lucky one to receive the windfall. He and his father took Scott and Dale to Frisborough on the Saturday to watch Peter Duncan play a blinder in Town's 1–1 draw.

The goalkeeper showed them round the ground afterwards. When he heard of Gary's plight, he went straight into the manager's office and emerged smiling with a handful of notes, enough to cover the cost of Gary's place.

'This money should tip the balance in Gary's favour,' he winked at them. 'His mother won't have to find another penny. Problem solved! He'll be there, you mark my words.'

He was right too. Mrs Clarke was persuaded, reluctantly, to accept the Club's gift and could no longer refuse to let Gary go.

So a smiling Gary joined the rest of the excited footballers on Thursday morning, as they waited impatiently to load their suitcases into the coach outside the school, before scrummaging for the best seats near the back.

With Mr Kenning and Mr Turner settling down at the front, the lads waved madly to the people on the pavement and cheered as the small coach began to pull away and chug off down the road.

'We're on our way!' shouted Jeff above the din. 'Let's go! Let's get at 'em!'

'Who?' Scott demanded.

'Bradbury first, and then the rest,' he laughed. 'Sandford are now on Tour.'

'On Tour! On Tour!' They all took up the chant and the coach echoed to the sound as it left the village behind on the first leg of its journey to Waverley.

3 Into Action

Mr Kenning intended to have every member of the squad in action against Bradbury School so that they would all immediately feel part of the Tour.

'You know your positions, so start to think about the game ahead,' he told them, trying to keep his balance in the aisle as the coach swayed along the country roads.

It was hardly necessary to say that as he knew it had been in their minds for days, at the expense of careless classwork, but he wanted to curb their excitement and create the right sort of mood.

'We're nearly there now. Remember that you're not just representing your school on this Tour, but Sandford village itself and the whole Frisborough area. So let's give a good account of ourselves.'

He left them to their own chatter to return to his seat and check through the team sheet with the Headmaster.

It read:

Ricky Collier

Sammy King   Scott Peters   Andrew Fisher   Paul Curtis

Dean Walters   Jeff Thompson (capt)   Graham Ford

David Woodward   Gary Clarke   Dale Gregson

Subs: Jimmy McDowell, Alan Clayton, John Robinson,

Robin Tainton, Ian Freeman

Jimmy, Alan and John would all normally be included in Sandford's full-strength side, but they would have their turn in the second half, along with keeper Robin and the versatile Ian. The teacher looked back at Gary, absorbed in his comic, and wondered how he was going to perform, and behave, during the Tour. He usually managed to leave his mark somehow or other!

Soon they were piling out of the coach, relieved to be able to stretch their legs at last. This was a novel experience for everybody, a real away match, already a long way from home.

'Just like travelling to play a European Cup-tie,' gabbled Dale, surveying their new surroundings.

But instead of entering some vast concrete soccer stadium, they were warmly welcomed by the Bradbury sports master,

and led past the small school pitch to a cloakroom to change.

'We've got some lunch laid on for you after the match, boys,' he informed them.

'Hey, hear that?' said Scott, poking Jeff in the ribs. 'Great, I'm starving.'

'You always are. I saw you stuffing yourself with sweets on the coach.'

Scott ignored the jibe. 'Better than the orange and biscuits we sometimes get after a game, if we're lucky.'

'Don't go mad about it,' Graham interrupted. 'It'll only be a school dinner, not a Cup Final banquet!'

The green shirts of the local lads emerged and the two teams took to the field, Sandford proudly wearing their striking all-red kit.

They used the warm-up period to try and remove the stiffness from their bodies after the journey. But despite their efforts and determination to make a good start, it quickly became obvious that something was wrong when the game kicked off.

The team failed to settle into its usual smooth rhythm, their passing was wayward, and they were being made to look sluggish and wooden by the lively home side.

Mr Kenning could hardly believe his eyes. 'They're all over the place!' he exclaimed, shaking his head. 'I've never seen them look so disorganized.'

'They'll soon get going once they've found their feet after all the travelling,' Mr Turner replied hopefully.

After only ten minutes, however, Sandford found themselves two goals down. The situation might well have been worse but for Ricky's alertness and a lucky bounce off the woodwork. Apart from restarting the game twice, Gary had not yet touched the ball as they had scarcely ventured into Bradbury's half.

Their young full back, Sammy King, a very promising player, was finding life difficult against a hard running left winger with excellent close dribbling skills, and both goals had originated from this area. With Dean Walters also not very experienced, Sandford's right flank looked vulnerable every time Bradbury advanced.

But it was a problem the team had to cope with themselves to avoid being swamped, and Jeff, as captain, took the responsibility to stay back more and support his defenders. He yelled encouragement to everybody to keep their heads up and play their way back into form. One of his more powerful clearances gave right winger David Woodward the chance to sprint away down the line.

With Bradbury committed to the attack, David found himself, unexpectedly, with space in which to manoeuvre and he ran menacingly towards goal. He easily side-stepped the first casual challenge and then, looking up, saw fellow winger Dale taking up a good position on the edge of the penalty area.

He hit across a low, accurate centre and Dale moved to meet it, controlling the ball with a skilful first touch. Before any defender could close up on him, Dale shot quickly, despite being on his weaker right foot. He struck it well, however, and was about to leap up in celebration when the keeper made a fine save, low to his left on the six-yard line, turning the ball away for a corner.

'Great try, Dale!' shouted Jeff, steaming upfield. 'That's given 'em something to think about now.'

Sandford were in business at last as an attacking force!

From that point on they began to play the better football and exert spells of pressure on the Bradbury goal. The moves started to flow in the entertaining Sandford style, defenders often coming up to add their weight to the attack when the chance arose. From one such raid down the wing, Paul and Dale swapped neat one-two passes before the left back sent a curling, skimming shot across the face of the yawning goal. But no-one was on hand to provide the vital finishing touch.

With Scott and Andrew again looking more assured at the heart of the defence, Bradbury posed little further threat. But try as they might, Sandford could find no way past the agile home keeper. His best save came just before the end of the 25-minute first half, when Gary suddenly popped up to stab a close range effort

almost over the line. But the keeper's quick reflexes allowed him to knock the ball out of danger.

As the whistle signalled the brief interval, they were still trailing by the two goals that their stumbling start had cost them.

'OK, lads, take a well deserved breather,' Mr Kenning greeted them. 'We've seen the best of them now and you've weathered the storm. You're well on top and the goals will come with a bit of luck.'

He praised the five players who were coming off, with a special word to Sammy who had handled the winger quite well towards the end. Jimmy McDowell, just a year older than Sammy, replaced him to play behind John, with Ian and Robin exchanging places with Andrew and Ricky respectively. Somewhat reluctantly, the teacher rested Gary in favour of Alan's extra height and power up front.

'C'mon, let's get at 'em again,' came Jeff's usual rallying cry as his reshaped team began the second half, full of optimism.

44

They continued to press forward, searching and probing for the much needed breakthrough. They had to be patient, but it came eventually when David collected John's throw-in and pushed the ball quickly inside into Alan's stride. The centre-forward bustled through one tackle and hit the ball firmly and decisively past the advancing keeper into the far corner of the net.

Sandford's spirits soared even higher but the goal also served to make Bradbury battle harder to protect their slender advantage. The last ten minutes were played at a cracking pace with both goals surviving narrow escapes.

A seemingly certain equalizer from Graham was kicked off the line, and soon afterwards at the other end Sandford suffered an agonizing goal-mouth scramble. The ball ricocheted among a tangle of limbs and bodies, like on a pin-ball machine, until Robin bravely claimed it from the thrashing feet.

But with Jimmy snuffing out the danger from the tricky winger, marking tightly and not allowing him space to turn with the ball and run at him, the home team created few real chances and had to rely on their defence to keep Sandford at bay. They managed to do this thanks mostly to the goalkeeper, and the game ended with their goal under siege but still intact.

Despite their excellent recovery, it was a disappointing 2–1 defeat for Sandford, but they could take some comfort from a good overall performance. The boys were downcast, though not too disheartened by the result.

'We'd have beaten them at home,' reasoned Graham, after they had changed and were waiting to enter the dining hall. 'We deserved a draw at least.'

The others agreed, but Jeff was quick to point out the difference. 'Possibly, but it goes to show how much tougher it is on Tour.'

He spoke as though he were the veteran of many similar trips. 'We've got to work together like a good Tour party should and see we don't make the same mistakes again. We got caught cold at the start.'

He looked around to check that they were all listening. 'We want to make this Tour a success. Right?'

'Right!' they chorused.

The shock defeat had served, if anything, to strengthen the spirit within the squad and make them even more determined to do well in the games ahead.

After all, they still had plenty to look forward to – including the welcome hot meal, especially prepared for a group of hungry young footballers!

'Anyone would think we hadn't had enough exercise already today,' Dale complained, half-heartedly, as he stumbled down the steep rocky path.

'Better than it was going up though,' sighed Jimmy.

'Oh, stop moaning,' John cut in. 'It's all good fitness training.'

'I felt fitter before we climbed right up there,' Dale answered back, looking over his shoulder at the ridge high above them.

No sooner had the boys arrived at the

Waverley hostel than the teachers ordered them into their walking boots for a brisk trek up to the top of the hill.

'It'll blow a few cobwebs away and work up a good appetite for tea,' Mr Kenning had predicted.

Scott had made them all laugh when he risked the reply, 'I'll wait here for you then. I've already got a good appetite!'

The slog upwards had made even the fittest of them puff and pant, and pause for breathers.

'I reckon they're trying to wear us out to make us sleep tonight,' Dale went on. 'Well, we'll see about that!'

The boys around him grinned at the thought.

'Yeah, we're going to have some great fun in those dormitories,' David laughed.

'Hey! That reminds me,' Paul added suddenly. 'It's April Fool's Day tomorrow, you know.'

They looked at one another, eyes glinting in anticipation.

'Magic!' Dale chortled. 'It's going to be a riot in a place like that. Anything could happen!'

Sandford were sharing the hostel with another football party from West Norton school, accommodated in small, neat rooms, each containing four bunk beds. They met up in the common room before the evening meal, and were introduced to the two instructors on the staff.

Steve and Colin, as they preferred to be known, soon became firm favourites with the children, always being willing to listen to a joke or join in with a bit of fun.

Steve, in fact, nearly deafened everybody by sneaking back into the room with the hostel's enormous metal dinner gong and making them jump sky-high when he gave it an almighty crash with the mallet.

'Tea-time,' he announced, with great amusement at their fright.

The evening saw Sandford enjoying a vigorous session in the Waverley swimming baths, and by the time they arrived back at the hostel they all knew that they had been through a very full day.

'They do look pretty tired at last,' Mr Turner observed. 'Perhaps they will get a good night's sleep.'

'I doubt it,' Mr Kenning smiled. 'I'm sure

they've got other ideas. But there again, so have we . . .'

The two men exchanged a wink of conspiracy.

The top bunks caused a few problems when it was nearly time for lights-out.

'You need to be an Olympic athlete to get up into these,' Dale joked, as he made several unsuccessful attempts to clamber into his bunk above a smirking Paul.

'High jumper, you mean?' he suggested.

'Pole vaulter!' came back the strangled reply as Dale finally struggled up.

Then his face suddenly reappeared over the edge. 'Er, Paul, my old mate, the next question is – how do I get back down again?'

Weariness claimed a few victims as some boys fell asleep almost immediately, despite the noises all around them. Talking, joking, laughing and banging on walls in between rooms continued for some time until regular teacher patrols and threats had their effect and calmed things down. Finally, even persistent chatterers like Dale and Scott could keep their eyes open no longer.

Eventually, all seemed quiet – Sandford's first busy day on Tour was over.

4 April Capers

CRASH . . . BOI-INNGGG . . . CLASH . . . DOI-INNGGG . . .

The gong's echoing and reverberating din shattered the morning stillness and shocked the boys out of their fitful slumbers. Its murderous noise was simply impossible to ignore.

Dazed and half-asleep, the boys tumbled out of bunks and fumbled for footwear in the gloomy confusion of their unfamiliar rooms, amid a babble of raised, startled voices.

'What's happening?'

'What is it?'

'Dunno.'

'It's that flippin' gong again.'

'At this time!'

'Where's my slippers?'

'What time is it?'

'It's only six o'clock.'

'What idiot's banging the gong at this time of the night?'

They soon found out. Mr Kenning's voice boomed above all their grumbles and questions.

'Come on. All of you. Time to get up. Straightaway. No messing about. Up and dressed. We're going out for an early morning hill-walk before breakfast.'

After their rude awakening this last stunning piece of news took a few moments to sink in, but then it brought howls of protest from them. All too late, however. The teacher had gone, leaving his parting commands hanging in the air . . .

'Hurry it up. You can get washed later. Jeans, boots, jumpers and coats on. We want you down in the yard in less than ten minutes.'

In the distance they could hear the West Norton boys being roused in similar abrupt fashion by one of their teachers.

Apart from moaning and groaning, there

did not seem much they could do about the situation. In dismay, and in between yawns, they began slowly and reluctantly to change from pyjamas into walking gear.

'This is ridiculous!' grimaced Andrew as he struggled into his walking boots in the corridor. 'They never said anything about this torture last night.'

'They didn't dare!' came back a reply.

At this point, Mr Turner breezed through to chase up the slowcoaches. 'Come on, out you all go. Get a move on there. Everybody downstairs in two minutes.'

Resigned to their fate, they shrugged their shoulders, gave heavy sighs and trudged down the steps and out of the building to stand and shiver in the chilly dawn air.

'Brrr! It's freezing!' Dale gasped.

Both sets of boys milled about in the yard in dishevelled disarray, feeling very sorry for themselves. As the minutes passed they grew more restless and mutinous. There was no sign of the teachers.

'C'mon, where are they?' challenged a West Norton lad. 'They drag us out of our warm beds, make us dress at the double and then keep us hanging around in the cold.'

'This is getting beyond a joke . . .' began

Paul. He stopped. The last word jarred his memory. 'Hey! Remember what day it is . . . something funny's going on here.'

'Well, I don't find it very hilarious,' Dale muttered.

The same awful thought seeped into everybody's mind.

'They wouldn't do that, surely . . . would they?' someone faltered.

As if in answer, several windows on the upper floor flew open and the heads of the instructors and all their teachers appeared.

'Sorry, lads,' Colin called out cheerily and unsympathetically. 'Go back to bed. We don't feel like going for a walk now.'

His words were swiftly followed by a loud chorus of 'April Fool!' and waves of farewell before the windows slammed shut once more. They just escaped all the jeers and complaints that were hurled their way from below.

The boys gradually slouched sheepishly

back inside. Their beds were now cold and uninviting, and everyone was too much on their guard to fall for any more practical jokes. Besides, every trick seemed puny in comparison with the gong hoax. It didn't help that some laughter could still be heard from the teachers' rooms.

'We can't let them get away with it,' Paul demanded. 'We'll be a laughing-stock back at school when the others hear about it.'

'We've got to do something for revenge,' cried Scott helplessly.

'Something really good,' Dale insisted.

'Well, we can play some little jokes on them to make them think we're getting our own back,' Ricky decided, 'but we need something big. They've sure asked for it. Let's see now . . .'

The final Sevens practice was due to take place in the afternoon, when the selection of the 'A' and 'B' teams for the Festival would be announced. Before that, however, the morning was given over to a sight-seeing tour of the old market town of Waverley, with its ancient buildings and ruined castle perched high on the hillside above them.

The boys had to suffer a lecture on church architecture from the Headmaster, but the

morning was sunny and they consoled themselves with thoughts of their pals bent over their desks working back at school. Finally they toiled up the narrow, steep lane towards the castle gates.

'Phew, I'd have been too tired to fight after charging all the way up here,' Paul wheezed.

'It must have been impregnable,' Alan reflected.

'Must have been *what*?' gaped Jimmy.

'Hard to attack and conquer,' Alan translated. 'Shall I spell it for you?'

'Don't bother,' the full back grinned. 'Sounds a bit like our defence when I'm playing!'

The guide made the visit very interesting, telling them about the battles fought there and showing them examples of armour and weapons. He also led them down to the deep, dark dungeons, where Dale suggested anyone who put through his own goal should be sent.

From there they climbed up the spiral stone stairway to the top of the tower where they were rewarded by a fabulous view for miles around.

'There's the hostel,' Sammy pointed out.

'And the recreation ground next to it, where we'll be this afternoon,' John added.

'Look over there too,' Jeff commanded, his arm outstretched. 'That's where it all happens tomorrow.'

They could see the Sevens pitches marked out on the sprawling green playing fields of a large secondary school.

'That's what we're here for,' he breathed in excitement. 'Let's get to that practice.'

They scuttled back down to wait by the ticket office for everyone to reassemble, eager for more soccer action.

It was only as the party straggled along the road leading to the hostel that Ricky suddenly exclaimed, 'Where's Gary?'

Everyone looked round and added their own comments.

'Haven't seen him since the castle.'

'Nor have I.'

'Typical! Trust Gary to get himself lost.'

The teachers groaned in dismay and shared the same thought, 'It would have to be Gary, of all people!'

They conferred briefly, then Mr Kenning looked at his watch. 'Time's getting on,' he announced, 'it's no use all of us going back to look for him. I'll find him while Mr Turner takes you in for lunch. I'll join you later.'

'Are you going all the way back up that hill to the castle?' asked Dale.

Mr Kenning grimaced. 'If I have to. Gary's probably up there waiting for us, though I don't suppose he's worried. I'm sure I counted you all properly before we left as well.'

They parted company, but Gary was nowhere to be seen. By the time the teacher
had trudged back up to the castle, the
church clock was chiming out mid-day and
he felt rather hot and bothered.

'Where on earth could the boy have got
to?' he mouthed silently.

The man at the ticket office reported no
sign of any stray boy, but then seemed to
remember something.

'Ah, would you be Mr Kenning? Some
boys did ask me earlier to give you this
envelope if you called back. Can't think
why.'

Mr Kenning took the envelope with rising
suspicion. Tearing it open, he guessed what
was written on the note paper before he
read it:

APRIL FOOL!! THE EQUALIZER!

He gazed at the printed capital letters for
ages, picturing Gary sitting at the dining
table with the rest of them. They would
all be laughing their heads off at the way

they had hidden him somewhere until the trap had been sprung.

He then remembered the twelve o'clock chimes and allowed himself a little smile too at their expense . . .

'Goal ruled offside!' he murmured.

The practice session went well, with everyone in good spirits after the morning's fun, all hoping they might be chosen for the stronger 'A' team. They had already experimented at school with several different line-ups, but Mr Kenning had not yet made his final decision known.

He had found the choice of substitute for the 'A's to be the trickiest. The boy needed to be worth his place in the team yet might be wasted on the touchline for much of the time. In the end Gary seemed the best option. He was the kind of player that Mr Kenning could bring on in the hope of providing a moment of inspiration, of individual flair, that might swing a game their way. His mind made up, he called the players together and sat them down.

'Whether you play in the "A" or the "B" team,' Mr Kenning began cautiously to lessen any disappointment, 'you're guaranteed a great day's football with at least three matches in your first group.'

As he announced the names and gave them further details, the two sides took shape as follows in a loose 3–1–2 formation, which they had used successfully in the past.

'A' Team

Ricky Collier

David Woodward   Scott Peters   Paul Curtis

Jeff Thompson (Capt)

Graham Ford   Dale Gregson

Sub: Gary Clarke

'B' Team

Robin Tainton

Jimmy McDowell   Andrew Fisher   Dean Walters

John Robinson (Capt)

Alan Clayton   Ian Freeman

Sub: Sammy King

The two major surprises were Alan playing for the 'B's where he would be a great boost to their chances, and David chosen as wing defence in the 'A' team, rather than as a forward. He was just happy to be picked to play anywhere and it certainly gave the 'A's a very exciting, attacking look.

In the couple of practice matches that followed, the teacher encouraged all of them to move up and down the pitch as the game dictated, helping each other in defence and

in attack. The key people in the sides were the two captains, Jeff and John, in mid-field, with the important link job to perform. They had to do a tremendous amount of running but both had the limitless energy and enthusiasm to excel in the role.

Each time the 'A's only just pipped their friends, proving how difficult the second team were going to be to beat.

'See you in the Final tomorrow,' they joked afterwards.

The evening was free for them to do as they wished. Some stayed indoors to watch the hostel's television or play table tennis, but most of them trotted back to the recreation ground to have a friendly kick-about with the West Norton footballers.

Soon their game was interrupted by the arrival of a gang of boys from the local school who demanded to join in.

Nobody minded at first until Waverley began to brag about how they were going to thrash all the 'foreigners' at the Festival.

'Who do they think they're calling foreigners?' John protested. 'I can see we shall have to show them a thing or two tomorrow.'

But the locals seemed determined to make an impression, one way or another. They began to push and shove, dig their elbows in and make clumsy, crude tackles and the game grew more heated.

'Hey, watch it!' Jeff warned as somebody tried to trip him after he'd passed the ball. 'Just cool it, will you.'

'Can't take it, eh?' his opponent taunted. 'There'll be some more of this to come tomorrow.'

'You must be mad then,' Jeff retorted, 'if you'd rather play dirty than play football.'

But the rough stuff continued and Jeff was concerned that someone might get crocked and have to miss the Festival altogether. He couldn't stop the game, and they were all so involved in it that they hadn't realized how dark it had become until Mr Kenning came across to call them in.

They all needed a good night's sleep before the tournament!

But there was still time for Waverley to throw down a direct challenge.

A big, strongly-built boy called Mark, who had made it clear he was their captain, confronted Jeff. 'We saw you practising this afternoon and we don't rate you lot from Sandford much.'

Jeff held his glare and felt his fists clenching as others gathered round. Mark checked he had the support of his mates before continuing.

'We challenge you to a proper match here on Sunday afternoon, eleven-a-side. We'd like to give you a good hiding.'

'Who d'you think you are?' Scott cut in, moving forward menacingly. 'I'll give you a good hiding if you want one.'

Jeff pulled his friend back. 'Save it, Scotty. I'll deal with it.'

He may have been a year younger, but Scott knew he could look after himself and had taken an instant dislike to this boaster. He wanted to sort it out now!

Jeff realized, though, that this had been a deliberate plan to rile them so that they could not refuse the challenge without seeming scared. He needed time to think.

'Sure we'd like to play you,' he found himself answering, 'but I don't know if we can arrange it. We've got other things lined up on our Tour.'

Mark took this as a sign of weakness. 'A Tour!' he sneered. 'Big deal! You're just making excuses.'

Jeff was fighting hard to control his own temper, never mind Scott's.

'We'll play you, don't worry, some time. We'll let you know tomorrow if we can make Sunday.'

'OK,' Mark drawled. 'You run along and check with your precious teacher. We'll be waiting.'

As they trailed back to the hostel the boys were seething with rage.

'We've got to play them, Jeff,' urged Alan. 'We can't afford to back down over this.'

'It'd be a real grudge match,' Scott growled, almost rubbing his hands together. 'I've got a few scores to settle.'

'What are we doing on Sunday?' Gary asked.

'Walking the hills,' came back the reply.

'Then we'll have to cut it short and get back here to play them,' Scott demanded.

'We'll see Mr Kenning when we go in,' Jeff promised. 'We'll just have to convince him how important it is.'

'Tell him Sandford's reputation is at stake,' Ricky suggested, which made them smile again at last.

'He'll agree, I'm sure,' Jeff said more confidently. 'But let's concentrate on the Tournament first, that's our main aim.'

He gave them a wicked grin. 'You never know. We may tangle with Waverley there as well!'

Jeff could not imagine as he spoke these words just how closely the opposing fortunes of Waverley and Sandford schools would be bound up together over the coming crucial weekend . . .

5   Football Festival

'Crikey! We don't have to play all this lot, do we?' gasped Paul. 'We shall be here all week, never mind all day.'

'I hope not,' Jimmy choked, pointing out one six-foot-tall footballer. 'I wouldn't fancy tackling him for a start.'

There were dozens of teams and hundreds of players milling around the school grounds. Shirts of every colour and design dazzled the eye, some plain, others striped and patterned with all kinds of fancy trimmings.

The boys knew of course that this Football Festival was organized for several different age groups, from primary upwards. The best schools from all over the region had been invited. It was planned as an end of season showpiece Tournament to reflect the high standard of schoolboy football and everyone felt a special thrill

to be taking part in such a major event.

'No wonder they need so many Sevens pitches,' Ricky said in amazement.

'All these spectators too!' David whistled. 'If anybody wanders off, he'll never be seen again.'

'Have to keep a watch on Gary, then!' Dale added with a grin.

Mr Kenning threaded his way through the crush near the school building to find out the vital information – which groups the two Sandford teams had been drawn in.

Sixteen teams made up the primary section, including some 'B' sides. They were arranged firstly in groups of four to play each other for league points. The group winners would then later contest the knock-out semi-finals for the honoured places in the Grand Final itself.

'Non-stop football all day – what could be better!' Jeff wondered out loud and then shouted, 'Hey! Look who's here too.'

They followed his direction and spotted the familiar face.

Simon Walsh, Tanby's soccer captain, heard their greetings, and the whole Tanby squad came across to join them.

'Made it at last!' Simon exclaimed. 'Thought we were going to miss the start. What a rush!'

'Had to get up at the crack of dawn, we're all still yawning,' Kevin Baker, their excellent goalkeeper, put in.

Sandford enjoyed a sense of superiority with already being based at Waverley.

'Yeah, we've had a long journey too,' Paul sympathized in jest. 'We had to walk all the way up the lane from the hostel!'

'Your eyes will still be closed when all the shots fly past you,' Ricky teased his opposite number.

'No chance,' Kevin retorted. 'We're here to win. We haven't come all this way for nothing, you know.'

Their rival banter was interrupted by Mr Kenning's return.

'Are we with Waverley?' Scott couldn't keep from bursting out.

'No, not yet. But the "A"s are with some new friends – your first match is against West Norton!'

'Oh, no!' came the chorus.

They had dreaded that happening. All the same, from what they had seen on the recreation ground Sandford still fancied their chances against them.

'You're also with a school called Havendon and a "B" side from Market Peyton,' Mr Kenning continued, as his own 'B's grew impatient.

'What about us?' asked John.

'Hold on. I haven't forgotten you. In your group are Church Fentley, Bridgeford and . . .' he paused and smiled, '. . . somebody called Tanby, whoever they are!'

A huge cheer went up – from both camps.

The times of their games often clashed so Mr Turner took charge of the 'B' side, hurrying them to change into their freshly laundered red kit ready for the opening -match.

John christened it the 'Battle of the Fords' and it was indeed a fast and furious game, starting at a cracking pace as both they and Bridgeford thirsted to taste first blood.

It was John in fact who showed his team the way by shooting them ahead, blasting the ball home from just outside the keeper's prohibited semi-circular area.

But by half-time the lead was reversed, with central defender Andrew Fisher at the heart of a controversy. His appeals to the referee that the scorer of the equalizing goal had handled the ball before netting were ignored and this upset his concentration.

With no offside rule being applied in seven-a-side, it was important for defenders to prevent the attackers from sneaking round goal-side of them. Andrew,

still annoyed over the previous incident, allowed himself to be caught out in this way when the ball was punted over his head to send his opponent clear. Robin was given no chance to stop them going 2–1 behind.

'Keep your mind on the game all the time,' the Headmaster told him at the break. 'Remember, the referee is always right – even when you think he's wrong. He's the one who makes the decisions and you must accept them straightaway.'

'Sorry,' Andrew apologized to his team-mates for his uncharacteristic lapse. 'It won't happen again.'

To his credit, he held the defence together under second half pressure. This gave Robin better protection, until Sandford began to play some more controlled football. It earned them a respectable 2–2 draw, and one point, when Alan's snap shot finished off a fine move up the left wing, just before the end of the seven minute period.

'Ah well,' John reflected, 'it could have been worse and there's still two games to go. I wonder how the "A"s are getting on?'

Their game with West Norton was just coming to a close with Sandford leading comfortably 2-0, thanks to Dale's two second half goals. The match had been tensely fought in the first period, but then Sandford caught their hostel partners twice on the break as they pushed forward too eagerly.

Both teams had been dismayed to have to line up against each other. But Jeff pointed out before the kick-off, 'It's either them or us now. We can't afford to be soft on them. We'll make friends again afterwards!'

Now cruising home, David took time off from his defensive duties to rattle the crossbar with a long-range drive. It proved to be the last action of the game and left him well pleased with his performance in the unaccustomed position.

'Great!' Jeff slapped him on the back. 'Jimmy will have to watch out for his full back place.'

'No fear! I enjoy playing on the wing too much, but on a small pitch like this I can still get up in the attack quite a lot.'

'I noticed,' Ricky remarked dryly. 'I had to call you back a few times when you were wandering about up there and we were a bit stretched for cover in defence.'

West Norton hid their disappointment, but knew now that they faced an uphill task in trying to qualify for the semi-finals. Meanwhile, Havendon, the other main contenders, had showed their paces by demolishing the Market Peyton 'B' side 4-1, and were Sandford's next hurdle.

There had been no contact yet with Waverley, but Sandford heard on the grapevine that they had opened their account with a crushing 5–0 victory.

'They do sound a bit useful,' Graham offered.

'We'll see,' was Jeff's only reaction.

They prepared carefully for the Havendon match, knowing that the winners would have an excellent chance of going through. Mr Kenning emphasized to the defenders the necessity to fill in for each other when one of them moved forward, especially if Scott left his post in the middle. He made sure David appreciated this too.

The game proved, in fact, how well they were knitting together as a unit, running and working hard for each other all over the pitch. By intelligent movement, they constantly created extra space for the player on the ball and supported him in case he lost it.

Their neat football enabled them to hold a slim, one goal advantage at half-time, through a smart interpassing move between Dale and his fellow striker. It allowed Graham to slip the ball under the keeper's body before veering away to avoid straying into his area.

But Havendon pressed hard afterwards for the equalizer, causing Ricky to become the star turn with two inspired saves to keep their noses in front.

Mr Kenning considered bringing Gary into the action but decided not to disrupt the side's rhythm, especially as Gary's attention seemed to be more on the neighbouring pitch where an Under-15 match was in progress.

'Come on, Gary, watch our game, not that one. Be aware of what's happening.'

Gary glanced back just in time to see his team's defence finally crack, despite Ricky's valiant attempt to stop the wickedly-deflected shot from spinning over the line.

The setback increased the teacher's irritation with Gary's attitude. He had missed the goal himself by looking around at the boy. 'He's got to show more interest,' Mr Kenning sighed. 'If only for his own sake. I'll see that he plays part of the next game to perk him up.'

Neither side could find the way through to goal again, leaving the score tied at 1–1, honours even after an enthralling match.

'Three points each now,' Jeff remarked as they reassessed their position. 'Looks like goal difference might be the deciding factor in the end.'

'Could be,' Graham agreed, 'but we've got the easier game against that "B" team. West Norton have just put three more past them.'

'That's right, Havendon won't find the West lads a pushover,' Scott predicted to boost their confidence.

'We can't rely on that, though,' David checked them. 'We've just got to make sure we score plenty of goals ourselves to wrap it up.'

Jeff sized the situation up. 'Well, let's hope so, but it won't be that simple, I bet. They won't want to lose by a big score again.'

Unfortunately, Sandford's own 'B' side were finding life hard too, trailing 0–2 at

half-time to an impressive Church Fentley outfit.

Once again they had left themselves too much to do in the final seven minutes. They proved good enough not to give away any more but, in attack, depended too heavily on Alan to provide their own goal punch. He did oblige, although with virtually the last kick of the match, and their 1–2 defeat put them sadly out of contention.

Sandford could no longer hope to catch Tanby, who had beaten both the other teams without conceding a goal. But their remaining game against their local rivals gave them a great incentive to go down fighting.

'We can still make it tough for Tanby,' John demanded, to keep his team's spirits up. 'Let's see if we can cause a shock by beating them and go out with a bang!'

There was a while to wait before then, though, and they took the chance to join up briefly with the 'A' team. They arrived at exactly the same moment as the 'A's had other visitors.

'Well?' The taunting question hung in the air between them.

'The game's on, if that's what you mean,' Jeff answered, trying to look cool and unconcerned as Mark's Waverley crew stood cockily in front of them. 'It's all fixed up.'

Fortunately Mr Kenning had not needed too much persuasion to agree to the extra match. It did seem to him an interesting bonus to the soccer Tour. But he would not have been so favourably inclined if he had known about the threats and the likelihood of rough play. He was soon to have second thoughts about it, in any case, when he saw Waverley in action for himself!

'We're out the first part of the day up on the hills, but we'll be back in time,' Jeff explained.

'Good job too,' Mark stated flatly. 'We thought you might chicken out of it. Just

don't tire yourselves out, that's all. We don't want you using that as an excuse.'

'Don't worry, we shan't be needing any excuses. Four o'clock OK?'

'We'll be there. Don't be late,' Mark said gruffly, and began to turn away.

'Hold on. What about a referee?' said Jeff.

'Referee! We don't want a ref,' Mark snapped. 'He'll only spoil things.'

Jeff was not going to fall for that. 'A proper game needs a proper ref or there'll be too much arguing.'

Mark could see that Jeff meant business and respected him for it. He shrugged his shoulders, 'OK. Not your teacher, though.'

'I didn't expect that. One of the hostel's instructors says he'll do it.'

'As long as he's not biased too. Anything to stop you belly-aching. Anyway, we've got better things to do than waste time here. Be seeing you.'

'Later today perhaps,' Scott threw in, but Waverley had the final word.

'Hope so,' one of them called back cheekily. 'We like easy games!'

'Drop it, Scott,' Jeff said quickly before he could take the matter further. 'We'll sort them out on the soccer pitch where it really counts.'

'They're obviously pretty good,' Graham judged. 'Too bad they have to be so big headed about it.'

'I can't wait to knock them down a peg or two,' Scott muttered, leaving no-one in any doubt how he felt about it.

'We've got to qualify first,' Jeff reminded him, 'and we're on in a minute. Come on.'

Mr Kenning too made sure they did not take anything for granted. Fortunes, he knew, could so easily change in football with some unlucky mistake or moment of brilliance.

A goal, after all, only needs one kick of the ball . . .

6 *Fluctuating Fortunes*

Cheered on by the 'B' team, Sandford went hard at the weaker Market Peyton side straight from the whistle, seeking the flood of goals to put them out of Havendon's reach.

But some of Waverley's digs were still rankling them and their football lacked its usual composed and fluent style.

'Come on, Sandford,' Mr Kenning encouraged. 'Settle down, think what you're doing.'

Market Peyton had reshuffled their 'B' team to good effect, tightening up the defence at the expense of posing little attacking threat. They fought for every ball like tigers, restricting Sandford to only a couple of decent chances, both screwed hurriedly wide of the target by Graham and Dale.

With the scoresheet blank at half-time, the teacher continued to urge them not to

panic but simply to keep plugging away and stay calm. He could see the tension in their faces. 'I'm bringing Gary on as an extra attacker. Let's see if he can provide the magic touch for us.'

As Gary quickly peeled off his outer clothing, he was as surprised as anyone to learn that Paul was making way for him.

'Show me how much you really want to play, Gary,' was Mr Kenning's only instruction to the substitute.

But before Gary could do anything, the teacher's gamble nearly backfired. A long clearance found a yawning hole in Sandford's left flank where Paul would normally have been stationed. To their alarm, an attacker appeared from nowhere and was beating Scott in the race for the ball.

It was a good job Ricky had been fully alert to the danger. He rocketed out of his area like an international sprinter and reached the ball a fraction ahead of the

attacker to hammer it away out of sight.

'Well played,' yelled Jeff in relief, applauding him, 'a great bit of sweeping up.'

The scare served to make them redouble their efforts but still they could not score. So much on top and yet so frustrating. Twice the woodwork was shaken and other shots were deflected wide, or blocked, or saved before Gary at last found the net. He slipped beautifully by two tackles and poked the ball past the keeper over the line.

But their joy was short lived. The referee judged that Gary had intruded into the area when shooting and promptly disallowed the goal!

'Now you've found the goal at last, let's have a real one,' John shouted from the sidelines.

The ice had been broken and something had to give.

Inside the final minute, they had still not abandoned hope as Jeff prepared to take a left wing corner. Everybody seemed marked up as he lashed the ball across and it passed straight through the keeper's area, with no-one able to enter and make contact. The loose ball sailed harmlessly away towards the right-hand touchline when David suddenly popped up and gathered it.

As the keeper scampered across his goalline to try and cover the new angle, he temporarily lost his positioning. David's low return shot flashed by his right hand, beating him for pace, into the large gap he had unwittingly left between himself and the far post. He turned in anguish to see the ball sneak inside it and nestle mockingly in the net behind him.

For a moment there was stunned silence before the 'A's whooped their relief and ran to lift the delighted David off his feet.

A game that began with Sandford expecting to score a hatful of goals finished with them utterly grateful for that single,

priceless, last-gasp effort that brought them two points for victory.

But their fate now hung in the balance. It was out of their control. Havendon already enjoyed a better goal tally, and now only needed to beat West Norton to finish top at Sandford's expense.

Some of the team intended to watch the crucial game, but Jeff led the others away. 'C'mon, there's nothing we can do here. We'll go and support the "B"s against Tanby.'

Tanby only required a point to clinch their semi-final place, but anticipated their hardest game yet. Sandford teams never gave in! They could expect no favours.

Tanby began an immediate heavy bombardment of Robin's goal, keeping him very busy but also playing him into top form. Young Sammy King had joined the defence for this game, with Dean moving forward to replace Ian Freeman. And Sammy soon showed his good positional sense, breaking up several attacks with neat, well-timed interceptions.

The defence looked more solid for his inclusion and, with Jimmy and Andrew both outstanding, they somehow prevented any first-half goals, which pleased them. Their mood changed, however, when Paul brought the news that Havendon were leading 1–0.

'If it stays like that, we're sunk,' Graham conceded, anxiously running a hand through his black curls.

But Jeff refused to believe their exit until the last ball had been kicked. 'Anything can happen yet. Just keep praying. C'mon, the "B"s,' he called out. 'Cheer us up with a goal.'

They did try. Both goals were peppered with long range pot-shots until Tanby gained the upper hand once more. Then, in the space of a minute, came two goals.

Against the run of play, it was Sandford who went ahead.

A defender stumbled over the ball right in front of Tanby's goal area, giving Alan a golden opportunity. Taken unawares by the gift, he snatched at the shot and Kevin Baker parried it, only to see the ball rebound out of his reach for Dean to slide it back into the goal.

Although their superior goal difference over Church Fentley could allow for a narrow defeat, Tanby's pride could not, and they were stung into decisive action. Taking advantage of the 'B' side's momentary loss of concentration after scoring, they swept straight down through the middle for Simon Walsh to give Robin the job of fishing the ball out of the netting.

Back on level terms at 1–1, both defences took a firmer grip and Sandford left the pitch at the end with heads held high.

Then they all raced towards the other pitch – but never reached it. Dale was coming slowly in their direction, head bowed, and they stopped and braced themselves for the bad news.

Jeff tried to hide his fears by greeting Dale first. 'The "B"s did well, held Tanby to a one-all draw . . .'

He trailed off.

'One each was it?' Dale nodded and then could no longer restrain himself.

'SNAP!!' he exclaimed, and punched his fist into the air, shouting again to make them understand. 'West did it for us – they equalized and put us through!'

He immediately found himself grabbed and pummelled by his delirious teammates.

'You little horror, playing a trick like that,' screamed Graham, pinning him on

the ground, 'I'm going to throttle you.'

'Later,' Jeff hauled him playfully off. 'Later. Save him for the finals first . . . and then we'll kill him!'

All the different age group competitions had now reached the semi-final stage. It gave a chance for the surviving teams to take some light refreshment before the climax of the Festival later in the afternoon.

The pairings in the primary section fell in Sandford's favour:

Sandford 'A' v. Dartingham
Tanby v. Waverley 'A'

'Wow! If we win our game, what a crunch Final it'll be!' David exclaimed. 'Tanby or Waverley. Great stuff!'

'Taking on Waverley twice in two days is a bit much, if you ask me,' Dale warned. 'We'd have no legs left.'

Graham kept their dreams of the Final within check. 'We've got to get past Dartingham first, and that's not going to be a piece of cake.'

'Somebody mention cake?' Scott asked hungrily, jolted up from his doze.

As the April sunshine bathed the playing fields, the two teams trotted on to the pitch, eager to resume their challenge for the Sevens title. Encouraging cries met them from the touchlines of, 'Come on the Reds!' and 'Fly, Darts, fly!'

The Darts flew indeed to their target. Within two minutes they had the ball

90

in the Sandford net, a firmly-struck shot bouncing awkwardly in front of Ricky's dive and eluding his flailing fingers. The first time that day that Sandford had found themselves in arrears.

Mr Kenning's eyes flittered away to where Gary was standing unconcerned in the middle of the 'B' team group, now changed and reduced to the ranks of spectators. He had already decided to use him again at half-time to keep the others on their toes, but it was very tempting to do so beforehand.

Paul, restored to the defence, was extra keen not to be substituted a second time in case it meant missing the Final itself. He gave everything he had to stifle the lad he was marking and barely allowed him a kick throughout the game. Equally, Scott and David gradually imposed their dominance over the opposing forwards, and Sandford forced their way back into the match.

Their reward came when Jeff provided a

perfect through-ball for Graham to move on to, and he gratefully smashed it well beyond the helpless keeper's dive.

All of a sudden it seemed a different game. Sandford now had the measure of the opposition and took full control of the proceedings.

Dale was the unlucky one to make way reluctantly for Gary and now feared for his place in the side, especially as Sandford's attacking play began to make Dartingham's gold shirts look a little tarnished.

They won an indirect free kick on the edge of the Darts' area when a defender, in desperation, ran into it to prevent a pass reaching Gary, who was waiting to turn the ball into an unguarded goal.

It was small consolation for Gary, but the team had practised a few tricks for this sort of opportunity. As Jeff stood over the ball with Graham at his side, the others dodged around to confuse and lose their markers. Two defenders were poised to lunge in to block Graham's expected drive. But when the whistle blew, Jeff calmly rolled the ball backwards instead, before he and Graham scattered.

Taken completely by surprise, there was nobody to challenge Scott who had quietly advanced to about five metres behind his captain. Scott swept in on the bobbling ball, nicely balanced, his weight over it to keep the shot down, and cracked it hard and low through the newly created gap.

With other bodies unsighting the keeper, the ball was bouncing back out of the net before he could even move for it. He simply stood, hands on hips, staring dejectedly at Sandford's noisy celebrations.

Dartingham offered little further resistance and were fortunate not to concede several more goals. Finally it was left to Gary to put the result beyond doubt. He jinked past two tentative tackles before squeezing the ball inside the keeper's near post, leaving only Ricky to feel any

sympathy for how the lad felt. There was no Peter Duncan here to rebuild his confidence.

News of the 3–1 scoreline was quickly conveyed to the other semi-finalists by the boys themselves, who wanted to discover their opponents in the Final as early as possible.

The teams were still locked in combat at 2–2, Tanby having equalized twice. Waverley did indeed look formidable. They were skilful but had several big, robust players who were not over-fussy about how they won the ball.

It had been a bruising encounter for Tanby with the referee tending to overlook the many petty fouls in an effort to keep the game flowing. He blew the final whistle.

'Two minutes each way extra time now,' Mr Kenning explained.

'Is that all?' Paul cried. 'There's hardly time to do anything.'

But there was time enough for Waverley

94

to settle the issue. A Tanby player was dispossessed by a high, painful tackle and the loose ball was struck fiercely past Kevin Baker.

'Foul!' Graham shouted, adding his voice to the many protests and looking round at Mr Kenning for confirmation.

The teacher made no comment, but his raised eyebrows were enough to signal what he thought of the referee's decision to allow the goal. He felt sorry for Tanby, as Waverley finished the game fresher and fitter than their luckless opponents, wearied at last by their long day of travelling and matches.

Mr Kenning and the Sandford party joined Tanby afterwards as they were left to lick their wounds and wonder what might have been.

The Tanby sports teacher showed Mr Kenning the lump on their top scorer's leg. The injury had blunted Tanby's attack. 'Some kid deliberately took a big swipe at him after he'd scored our first goal. It was disgraceful, the ref ought to have sent him off. They're welcome to their place in the Final if they want it that badly. I just hope your lads come out of it unscathed!'

The boys were equally upset about Waverley's strong-arm tactics.

'I don't envy you, Jeff, honestly,' Simon Walsh confessed. 'They're prepared to kick anything that moves.'

'I know. We've had a taste of it already,' Jeff grimaced, 'and we're playing them again tomorrow in a full game.'

Simon whistled. 'Phew! I'm glad I'm not in your boots then. You sure won't be able to call it a *friendly* match.'

Jeff forced a false laugh. 'No, you're right, but we'll have to see what happens today first.'

'Do us a favour, will you?' Simon pleaded, pulling his tracksuit top on. 'Go out and beat them for us. They don't deserve to win it.'

'We'll do our best,' Jeff promised. 'You can count on that. They might find they've bitten off more than they can chew this time.'

7 Final Act

After a certain amount of recovery period, the Festival organizers staged all the Grand Finals at the same time, the town of Waverley represented in many of them.

The primary team's noisy support created an exhilarating atmosphere to lift their players for one last great effort.

It helped stimulate Sandford too, but made them breathe deeply to steady their nerves.

'This is a real away match. I reckon we're playing against the crowd as well,' Paul commented.

Mr Kenning was concerned that they should not be overawed by the size of their task. 'Just ignore them, and play your normal game,' he advised. 'Don't allow yourself to be distracted and *don't*, on any account, get involved in any trouble.'

The teacher had not liked Waverley's

attitude and was already having serious misgivings about letting the Sunday match go ahead. Any bad feeling aroused today would be likely to carry over to their next meeting.

He looked around at their faces to satisfy himself that his stern warning had been clearly understood. 'Whatever they may try and do, I don't want to see any retaliation from you people. All right?'

They nodded agreement.

'Good. Lecture over, then. The best of luck to you. Waverley have some good players, a side can't just kick its way to success – it has to be able to play too. So let's go out there and show them how football really should be played.'

Gary's excellent goal had secured his place at left attack as expected, leaving Dale to hope that he might be called upon at some point in the longer match. The Final was to be ten minutes each way.

Waverley, in their blue and white striped

shirts, glared at Sandford before the start. And as the captains came together to toss up, Mark couldn't resist a final jibe. 'Suckers for punishment, aren't you? You're gonna cop it twice now.'

Jeff took no notice and shook hands with the referee instead, hoping that this one would be firm enough to clamp down on any unfair play.

Waverley immediately made their intentions clear. Gary was clattered to the ground quite deliberately by a wild, late tackle with no attempt to play the ball.

The whistle blew for a foul, and while the referee spoke to the offender, Gary rose stiffly but without complaint to his feet. Mr Kenning sighed with relief but he knew that Gary was the kind of boy to sulk rather than seek physical revenge. His main worry was whether such tactics would dampen his appetite for the game. He could so easily fade right out of the picture.

'That'll slow you down a bit,' Gary's

marker jeered when the referee was out of earshot, but he made no reply and continued to rub his shin.

Nothing came of the free kick, and indeed neither goal was seriously threatened for the first five minutes as the teams probed each other cautiously for possible weaknesses. Gary, in particular, received more than his fair share of the jostling, tripping and niggling fouls whenever he tried to dwell on the ball. Graham and Jeff, both more powerfully built, commanded greater respect. But at least Sandford were being given better protection by this referee than Tanby had experienced. He was more prepared to penalize the culprits.

Scott too, though, felt the wrath of his tongue once when he brought down an opponent who had tried unwisely to barge past him. He looked guiltily over towards Mr Kenning but the direct free kick nearly punished him far more dearly. He was grateful to Ricky for clinging on to the rasping drive low to his left.

Paul broke up the next spell of Waverley pressure and had the satisfaction of starting the move which led to the only goal of the first session. He carried the ball over the halfway line, itself a slightly brave and reckless act which risked receiving the

treatment, as Mark politely termed it. And he had the skill to ride one ill-judged sliding tackle. Before another player had the chance, he swung the ball right across to David on the opposite side as Sandford committed themselves to a full-scale attack.

This clever switch of play caught Waverley flat footed for a vital moment, and David used his winger's pace to take advantage of it. They recovered quickly, however, and blocked his way to goal, forcing him to check back and shield the ball.

He looked up for support and saw Graham's unselfish decoy run take a defender out of the middle. Carefully, he laid the ball inside for Jeff to fasten on to, and watched the skipper hammer it past the exposed keeper for his first goal of the tournament.

'A long time coming,' Jeff told himself as he accepted their congratulations, 'but well worth waiting for.'

It had been an excellent team goal – good passing, thoughtful movement and finished with deadly accuracy.

Waverley set about trying to restore their dented prestige with renewed vigour but Sandford's barrier held firm. The half ended with Gary again put on the seat of his pants by an illegal tackle from behind, which summed up Waverley's frustration and annoyance.

Gary had been allowed to make very little impression and Mr Kenning had to admit that this was no game for his more delicate skills. Dale was not much better equipped to handle the situation but he wanted to bring back his talented little winger.

'You've taken enough stick,' he sympathized as he broke the bad news while Gary was busy inspecting the damage underneath his socks.

Then the teacher shook his head. 'Aren't you wearing shin pads? If I'd noticed, you wouldn't have played at all. I don't know, you do ask for it sometimes. They'd have saved you from a lot of pain and some of those bruises.'

With further bits of advice and encouragement, he sent his 'A' team back on to finish the job.

'They're getting worried now,' Jeff pointed out. 'Look at their faces, they know we're on top.'

Despite this, though, Waverley hit them with a flurry of raids and a series of corners that were only cleared with difficulty. And at last the home side exhibited the kind of football that proved they really had no need to resort to their less desirable tactics.

The game was far from over. Sandford enjoyed a moment of great fortune when Ricky's fingertips took the sting out of a shot, and everyone had to watch anxiously

as the ball trickled towards the goal. Nobody could enter the area to deal with it, and as Ricky scrambled to his feet the ball spun to one side and clunked against the foot of the post. There it sat, waiting for the thankful goalkeeper to pick it up!

But soon after a breakaway and shot from Dale, Waverley did finally pierce Sandford's armour. The left winger stormed through a limp challenge from David, a rare glimpse of his defensive inexperience, and managed to beat Ricky with a well directed drive.

As spectators and players leapt around, Jeff realized the critical time had come. 'Keep it tight,' he ordered. 'We can't let them score again.'

Waverley were poised to go on the rampage and, believing that actions spoke louder than words, Jeff resolved to stamp his own authority back on the game. All feelings of weariness dropped away and he geared himself up, selecting his target.

Mark expected Sandford to crumble now, just like all the other teams did that they met. They had proved much better than he had given them credit for, but now the Final was there for the taking.

Straight from the kick-off his side nearly sealed it when they regained possession and sent a shot whizzing just over the crossbar. Only a matter of time, the captain thought, before they went ahead and won the match. Waverley quickly seized the ball again and Mark demanded it, standing on the centre spot and waving his players forward. He sensed the kill and advanced threateningly himself, deep into Sandford territory.

It felt as though he had run headlong into a brick wall!

Every bone in Mark's body was painfully jarred and, big lad that he was, he crumpled to the ground, all the breath knocked out of him.

He had tangled with Thompson the Terror and come out of the encounter very much second best.

Jeff had gone in like a tank with as powerful a tackle as anybody could ever remember. His full weight was behind the crunching contact that made the crowd gasp and the other players wince. No-one could complain, however. Jeff had met the ball fair and square, staggered away with it at his feet, and managed to play it out to Dale.

With their captain laid flat out and the team committed to an all-out attack, the route to Waverley's goal was barred only by one remaining defender.

Two against one, plus the goalkeeper, was a situation that Dale and Graham had practised endlessly at school and they rarely failed.

Dale held the ball until the very last moment, sacrificing himself to the lumbering defender, who was homing in like a guided missile to smear him out of the game. He flicked it on to Graham a fraction before being caught by the full force of the scything lunge. Unable to brace himself in time, he was sent flying up into the air.

Seeing that the other Sandford player was now in the clear, the referee sensibly played the advantage rule and didn't blow his whistle for the blatant foul. The desperate goalkeeper came haring right out of his area in the hope of making the attacker shoot hurriedly wide. But Graham kept his head, dummied and sidestepped the unbalanced charge, and then coolly slotted the ball into the vacant goal.

The scene around him was chaotic, with the keeper grounded, Dale and the defender entangled in a heap, Mark still only up on his knees, Jeff limping slightly and the rest of the Waverley team throwing themselves to the floor in despair.

Even Ricky came racing out to help Dale to his feet. 'Worth it,' came his shaky reply when it finally sunk in that Graham had scored from his pass.

The goal and Jeff's emphatic response had an obvious subduing effect on Waverley, and he was given a generous wide berth whenever the ball went near him. Mark certainly kept his distance, and all the steam and aggression leaked out of their performance.

But 2–1 is always a slender lead, and the last couple of minutes seemed like a lifetime to the Sandford party on the touchline. Those on the field, however, had no further doubts and threw their arms up in triumph at the final whistle.

Jeff managed to disengage himself from all the well-wishers and found Mark.

'No hard feelings,' he said, offering his hand, but Mark declined it, looking back at him blankly, his face drained of colour by all the effort and disappointment.

He almost choked on his words. 'You wait. You may have won today but it'll be a different story tomorrow. Four o'clock. We'll be there.'

It sounded more like a threat than a promise.

Jeff rejoined his friends and soon brightened up again.

'What a tackle!' they greeted him.

'I felt that myself,' said Simon Walsh, pulling a pained expression.

'We all did!' John laughed.

'That Mark didn't know what day it was when he got up!' Jimmy exclaimed.

'Tremendous, boys, a magnificent achievement,' the teacher joined in. 'You did Sandford proud today.'

Their excitement had still not subsided as they lined up soon afterwards with all the other winning teams to be awarded their individual souvenir medals. Jeff also received the Festival's pennant for the school to keep in its trophy cabinet and, grinning broadly, he held the flag aloft to loud applause.

'What a day! What a day!' was all Scott could repeat as he gazed down at his tightly-clutched medal. It somehow symbolized the success of a Tour that was still only halfway through.

The Saturday night treat was a trip to the cinema to enjoy a comedy film. They rocked in their seats with laughter, but the smile on the face of the day's hero had nothing to do with the film. Completely whacked from all his exertions, Jeff slept soundly right through it.

Nobody dared to disturb his contented dreams!

8 *Fighting Fit*

'Great fun last night, eh?' Dale nudged Paul, making him spill some of his orange.

'Watch it! I want to drink this, not wash my jeans with it.'

'What a riot!' Dale laughed, unconcerned. 'We caught them well and truly napping.'

'We sure did.' Paul needed little encouragement to relive the previous night's antics. 'I never expected it to work so well.'

Sandford's daring midnight raid on the unsuspecting West Norton dormitories had been their idea of a farewell present to thank them for their help in the tournament.

It was the last night of West Norton's stay, and Sandford felt they could not let them leave without throwing a bit of a party.

'We certainly gave them something else

to remember us by,' chuckled Dale again at the thought of it.

They had pretended to be asleep when Mr Kenning and Mr Turner made their occasional patrols along the corridor, barely managing to suppress their giggles when they overheard one of them comment that everywhere seemed suspiciously quiet.

But later, when the whole hostel was dark and silent, Dale gave each door a soft, signal knock. One by one, the boys crept out, pillows in hand, and followed him noiselessly down to West's rooms on the floor below.

Their soccer teamwork had rarely been better co-ordinated. With split-second timing, all the doors were thrown open and they charged in, jumping on to the sleep-drugged occupants of the bottom bunks and climbing up to those on the top, pummelling away with their pillows.

Their victims were quite helpless at first to resist the merciless onslaught, but

soon recovered from their surprise and
defended themselves equally forcefully.
Clothes, blankets and sheets, sleeping
bags and pillows were scattered and
strewn everywhere in a magnificent,
hilarious fight, which spilled out into
the corridor.

The noise was almost enough to waken
the town, and when the teachers arrived on the scene in dressing gowns
and slippers to switch on the lights, an
incredible tangled confusion of bedclothes
and dishevelled, half-naked bodies met
their eyes.

The instructors, to the boys' amazement
and gratitude, came to their rescue before
the teachers had a chance to bellow and
threaten, but even they seemed to be trying
hard not to laugh.

'High spirits, that's all,' Steve excused
their behaviour.

'You've got to let off a bit of steam after
a great day like they've just had,' Colin
backed him up.

In the end they escaped remarkably
lightly. The teachers merely insisted that
the guilty ones tidied up all the mess
and made the beds again properly before
being escorted back to their own rooms.
It had even been worth suffering all the
good-natured mocking and teasing from
the West Norton boys as they did so.

Now, as they sat enjoying their packed
lunches on the wind-swept ridgeway path
that followed the crest of the hills, they
remembered fondly their own particular
favourite moments of their successful
assault.

The spectacular views that lay before them on either side of the ridge, as the two valleys stretched away into the far distance, paled into insignificance beside their daydreams.

'The look on their faces . . .' David recalled with amusement.

'Pity they're off home,' Scott sighed, 'otherwise I'm sure they would have tried something on us tonight in revenge.'

'We'll have enough retaliation to cope with this afternoon,' Paul reminded him. 'You can bet your life that Waverley will be preparing something nasty for us to make up for yesterday's defeat.'

'I think I'd rather insure my life,' Dale replied, only half in jest. 'They don't take any prisoners when they tackle. Have I shown you my bruises from that clobbering I took?'

He was about to pull his trouser leg up yet again when Scott stopped him. 'Yeah, yeah, hundreds of times, everybody's seen

them,' he scoffed. 'You never let us forget it.'

'We all picked up a few souvenirs like yours in the course of duty,' David laughed.

Scott gave them a sly grin. 'But we paid a few back too. I know I did!'

'Don't worry, we can handle them whatever they try and do,' Alan chipped in, assuring anyone who may have been in doubt. 'They'll have to respect us a bit now they know they can't just knock us out of our stride.'

They heard Mr Turner urging them back on to their feet again.

'I only hope we're fit enough to face them after all this slogging along,' grunted Dale, pulling on his haversack, glad at least to feel it lighter now that his lunch was inside him rather than riding on his back.

'Up to the hill fort,' the Headmaster pointed out ahead. 'That's our goal.'

'Oh good!' whispered Dale cheekily to his near neighbours. 'Anybody brought a ball with them?'

They managed a none too serious groan as they set off towards the steep, sloping sides of the Iron Age hill fort. Cut into a layered series of mounds and ditches, it straddled the highest point on the hills.

'It feels like we're on top of the world up here!' David exclaimed, as he walked with a small group alongside Mr Kenning ahead of the trailing pack.

'I thought you were yesterday after you won the Sevens,' the teacher smiled.

He glanced back to where the Headmaster had halted the others to explain some landscape feature of geological interest.

'This is our chance,' Mr Kenning told the six boys. 'Up over the next rampart quickly.'

He had already outlined his plan to them and they spaced themselves out along the top of the bank. 'After last night's little escapade, you can now do battle again, but this time in the proper surroundings!'

They waited in anticipation as their friends approached the ditch below them.

'Now we'll show them why these forts were constructed like this,' the teacher said. 'If they want to go any further, they'll have to fight their way past us first. Get ready to challenge them, Jeff.'

The rest of the party grew suspicious as a line of bodies appeared menacingly above them.

'You cannot pass!' Jeff thundered, standing tall like some ancient tribal chief. 'I command you to retreat.'

'Huh! We'll see about that,' cried Graham, throwing down his bag and indicating to the others to do likewise.

'Charge!' he roared, and led a determined attack straight up the mound. But the steepness of the banking checked their momentum, and they laboured up the final couple of metres.

Off balance, they were easily repulsed by the more securely placed defenders, and they were sent slithering and rolling back down the slope into the ditch.

'This is not as easy as it looks,' Scott gasped, brushing off loose bits of grass and earth from his coat. 'C'mon, let's try again.'

They struggled back up but few met with any greater success. Only Sammy squirmed through the main barrier, while Gary and Robin managed to scramble round it by skirting its flanks, and they immediately joined forces with the defenders. David, though, was dragged down from his perch and now had the difficult task of attempting to win back his position.

It quickly became a matter of every man for himself as several more charges were launched. Soon the bank was a mass of grappling, wrestling tussles as they each tried to topple somebody else downwards. Even the two teachers occasionally found themselves hauled to the ground by weight of numbers. And everybody at some stage enjoyed having the upper hand near the top, defending the fort against the invaders.

Eventually, by common consent, a truce was called and they slumped on to the top of the rampart, breathing heavily and nursing the odd knock and graze without complaint.

'Wow!' Graham let out. 'That was some battle!'

They were all winded and needed time to cool down a little.

'Imagine what it must have been like two thousand years ago trying to capture one of these hill forts,' Mr Kenning began as he had everyone's attention. 'Having to carry your weapon and fight your way up over these defensive ramparts to reach the main camp right at the top.'

'Impossible!' David cried.

'Well, not quite, but even the Roman armies found them very difficult to conquer when they arrived here,' he explained.

'It's just like Waverley Castle in a way,' Paul realized. 'Built on the top of a hill with a view for miles so you can't get caught out by surprise.'

120

'Like West Norton last night!' Dale added to general laughter.

'It sure is easier fighting downhill than going up,' Jeff appreciated. 'The defenders have a terrific advantage.'

'It's a bit like playing soccer on a sloping pitch,' Andrew offered a comparison. 'Hard work when you're kicking up.'

'At least you know then you're going to change ends at half-time to make it fair. I don't reckon they'd swap round halfway through a battle!' Scott hooted.

'Talking of football, which you seem to do most of the time,' Mr Kenning said, 'let's have a good clean match this afternoon. I didn't like some of the things that went on yesterday.'

'There'll be no trouble from us,' Jeff promised. 'They started it the other day.'

'I'm just hoping they don't try and finish it as well, that's all,' Mr Kenning concluded. 'You know what I expect. I don't want to interfere with your game, but I shan't hesitate to stop it if it looks like getting out of hand.'

The possibility of that horrified them. It would be a terrible humiliation in front of Waverley if their teacher stepped in to protect them! They quickly put the thought out of their minds.

'Come on now,' Mr Turner announced. 'Time for a look round at the top, where the Ancient Britons once built their huts, before we make our way down.'

Down they did go eventually, but arrived back at the hostel later than intended, giving them little time to recover before preparing for the match. They had already spotted Waverley out on the recreation ground, kicking-in casually at one of the goals.

Mr Kenning had suggested they chose their own team for the challenge match, and discussions and arguments over places and tactics had lasted right through breakfast up to the time of setting out for the hill walk. Finally, after many changes of mind and alterations, Jeff scribbled down

the names that most of them agreed upon,
but laid them out in a different way than
usual.

Ricky

Jimmy Scott Andrew Paul

John Jeff

Gary Alan Graham Dale

Subs: David, Ian

'We'll try a 4–2–4 line-up for a change,'
Jeff decided, 'and see how it works with
Alan and Graham as a twin spearhead.
John and me can look after the midfield
mostly.'

The choice of Gary had been at Jeff's in-
sistence too. 'Gary's scored some incredible
goals this season for us and he's always
sub, so let's give him a chance,' he had
reasoned. 'Dave knows he'll come on some
time in the game.'

As they pulled on their spare all-white
kit, with their red strip still in the wash,
Gary hoped he would justify Jeff's faith in
him. The possibility of receiving more of the
treatment didn't bother him – anything was
better than simply standing about watching. Besides, Dean had lent him a pair of
shin pads!

Dean and the two younger boys, Robin and Sammy, had not been risked for this match, but they trotted out across to the pitch with the thirteen players to be greeted by a few jeers and cat-calls.

'You took your time,' Mark glowered.

'Give us a chance,' Jeff replied. 'We didn't go walking in our football boots, you know. It's only just gone four o'clock.'

'You're gonna be in no fit state to play anyway,' Mark taunted. 'We'll run you off the park today.'

'Don't bank on it, we're fighting fit,' Jeff called back, and then smiled to himself over what he'd said. They should be after their night-time raid and hillside battles!

But he had to admit privately that walking all those miles was not the ideal preparation for an important game like this.

He just had to hope that his team could last the pace . . .

9   *Sunday Soccer*

Before the kick-off, John drew Jeff's attention to the Waverley players grouped at the other end of the pitch.

'Have you seen those two giants they've got in their team?' he asked. 'They're massive. I reckon they're about thirteen at least.'

'Oh, come on. They wouldn't try and pull a trick like that,' Jeff replied.

'You want a bet. They're dying to get even with us. I wouldn't put anything past them.'

'I certainly don't remember them from the Sevens,' Jeff had to confess.

'Course not,' said John. 'Just look at the size of them. Dale could run through their legs. But what can we do about it?'

'Nothing,' Jeff answered simply. 'It's too late now. We'll just have to put up with it.'

Mr Kenning shared their concern and went across to question Mark. 'Is your teacher here with you?'

'No, he knows nothing about it. This is our own team.'

'So I see,' he said ironically, and he nodded towards the two boys who stood head and shoulders above the others. 'And you're all at the primary school?'

Mark reddened ever so slightly, but covered his embarrassment with a cheeky quip. 'Sure. Some are just big for their age, that's all.'

Mr Kenning looked at him doubtfully, but knew it was not worth pursuing the matter any further. He could not exactly demand to see their birth certificates!

'Don't worry,' Mark added hurriedly, as if to excuse them, 'those two ain't much good – a couple of cart horses really, you'll see.'

'Yes, we will,' Mr Kenning thought, returning to the touchline. 'More like a couple of cloggers, probably.'

He knew the boys would not thank him for making a scene, but he was reassured by Steve, the referee.

'Leave it to me,' the instructor said. 'I've refereed loads of games. They won't get away with anything during the match itself. I won't stand for any nonsense.'

Jeff conducted the brief team talk. 'Forget about the two giants. It doesn't matter how big they are, it's skill that counts.'

'Right!' Scott agreed. 'And you know what they say – the bigger they are, the harder they fall!'

He rolled up his sleeves in a business-like manner and they all took their places. They noticed that one of the Big 'Uns, as they called them, lined up at centre forward and the other in defence.

The game was away and Waverley soon mounted a series of penetrating attacks that had Sandford stretched and breathless within a few minutes. Most of the team were anchored in their own half helping

out in defence, leaving only Gary and Alan up front as targets.

But they somehow kept Waverley out and began to put together some useful moves themselves. Apart from minor infringements, the game had started trouble-free and the two Big 'Uns had made little impression. Pleased to have withstood the early pressure so well, Sandford relaxed their guard a moment and suffered the consequences.

A harmless looking centre flopped into the penalty area from the left and Andrew Fisher appeared to have it covered comfortably. But the big attacker was on to him more quickly than he had anticipated, and his threatening presence was enough to distract him. Andrew sliced across the ball instead of striking it cleanly, and as he tumbled to the ground, he watched in horror as the ball looped crazily over the stranded Ricky and dropped into the goal behind him.

Waverley mocked Andrew unsportingly, ruffling his hair as they ran past where he sat, head in hands, until Ricky and Jeff hauled him back on to his feet.

'Can't be helped,' Jeff tried to console him. 'Even the best professionals sometimes put through their own goal.'

'Were you pushed?' Ricky demanded, but Andrew shook his head, resisting the temptation to use that as an excuse.

He took the full blame upon himself. 'No, he never touched me. I just took my eye off the ball for a second, expecting to be flattened.'

'Don't let them put you off, Andy,' his captain urged. 'Go for the ball hard, make them keep out of your way.'

Andrew was relieved not to hear any criticism from his team-mates and Dale even brought a smile back to his face.

'Remember what I said at the castle,' the winger called out. 'That's you for a night in the dungeon!'

Andrew was determined not to let his error affect his play and he went into the next tackle as firmly as he could, against the Big 'Un too, and came successfully away with the ball.

'Well done, Andy,' Scott winked at him when he had cleared it upfield. 'That's shown him who's boss again.'

They battled on, a goal adrift, with Ricky still the busier of the two keepers. Once he was forced to race out of his area to kick clear a long through-ball, and then another save conceded a corner. From this, he was beaten by a header from the Big 'Un who out-jumped Scott for the ball. But it thudded against a post and rebounded into the crowded goalmouth. In the scramble that resulted, Ricky parried a shot from point-blank range, and both John and Paul blocked efforts on the line before Jimmy finally hoisted the ball out of danger.

At the other end, even someone with Alan's proven heading ability stood little chance against the second Big 'Un, making full use of his height advantage.

Jeff ordered a change of tactics. 'He's swallowing up everything in the air, but doesn't look too hot on the ground. Keep the ball on the deck more.'

The two youths were now having an increasing influence on the pattern of play but at least they were not throwing their extra weight about too much. The referee kept a firm grip on the game and when a heavier tackle did hit Gary unfairly from behind, Steve made it very clear to the offender that it would not be tolerated and that he risked being sent off.

Even so, whenever Dale or Gary tried to use their dribbling skills to good effect by running at the defence, they were usually given uncomfortably bumpy rides, which earned little more than frustrating free kicks.

It was from one of these, however, that Sandford's equalizer came.

From near the left touchline, Jeff drove the kick hard and low into the area, an awkward ball for any defence to deal with. Graham shaped to play it but at the last moment let it go through his legs to fool his marker. It was meant to run to Alan,

but unfortunately he wasn't expecting it either, and the ball passed through to Gary who had more time to see it coming. He struck it well, full on the instep, but the ball was skimming wide of the post until Dale stretched out a leg and deflected it firmly past the goalkeeper and between two covering defenders on the line.

The goal gave Sandford renewed strength and purpose, and they enjoyed a brief but rewarding period of supremacy which brought them their second, not long before half-time.

The move had built up along the right-hand side with Jimmy and John working the ball out to Gary. He tried to go outside the full back, lost the ball for a moment, and then managed to win it back to play it off quickly inside to Alan. The striker held the ball skilfully, shielding it with his body from Mark, who was snapping away at his ankles, before releasing it perfectly back into Gary's path down the wing.

Gary cut into the box, thought for a second about lofting it over to Graham who was shouting for it, but then ignored him. He preferred, as usual, to go all the way himself. He often wasted a chance by not passing and then losing possession, much to the others' annoyance. They accused him of greediness, but sometimes it paid off handsomely and all would be forgiven.

This time, as he drew his foot back to shoot, his legs were swept from underneath him by the Big 'Un's clumsy trip and he was sent crashing forward full-length along the ground. For a moment all he could see were dazzling white stars.

The cries of 'Penalty!' brought him back to his senses as the referee pointed, without hesitation, to the spot. Even Waverley could not argue about the decision and contented themselves with hurling abuse at their new recruit.

Jeff strode up out of habit to claim the ball but then, to everybody's amazement, promptly handed it over to Gary and told him to 'do a Duncan' on the Waverley keeper. Gary stood open-mouthed for several seconds, staring at him.

'Go on,' Jeff urged, 'you're our new penalty king. If Peter Duncan couldn't stop one, this poor kid's got no chance!'

Gary's face lit up. If he felt any nerves about taking the penalty, he certainly didn't show them. The possibility of missing it never entered his head.

Carefully and unhurriedly, he placed the ball on the penalty spot, looked up and caught the keeper's eye and gave him a mischievous grin. He then took a few steps back and waited for the whistle before loping in.

The keeper launched himself forward and to his right, even before Gary made contact. But to no avail. He was left clutching at thin air, as Gary's delicate chip sent the ball floating into the opposite corner of the net.

Gary held one arm aloft in triumph to receive the acclaim as the red-faced goalie collected the ball and hoofed it miserably back up the field.

Sandford were grateful to sink down at half-time for a couple of minutes rest, delighted with their 2–1 scoreline, but knowing there was still a long way to go. The match meant too much to Waverley for them meekly to accept another defeat.

Paul volunteered to stand down to allow Ian to play the full second half, and they braced themselves for Waverley's expected onslaught.

'For what we are about to receive . . .' murmured Dale.

It duly came. Sandford had everything thrown at them, with both Big 'Uns now

charging around in attack, but by a mixture
of fine defensive skills, occasional big boots
and moments of good luck they managed
to cling on to their narrow lead. Sandford's
own raids were rare, their best chance aris-
ing from a breakaway which relieved the
pressure temporarily, when Alan brought
a good save out of Waverley's mostly un-
employed goalkeeper.

The minutes ticked away, achingly
slowly for Sandford it seemed, but far
too quickly for the increasingly desperate home team. So near and yet still
so far. The strains and events of the
Tour, and shortage of revitalizing sleep
at night, were catching up on the Sandford
players and sapping their energy rapidly.

Jeff knew that he and his team were
flagging, and could see that John had
virtually run himself to a standstill. They
needed a fresh pair of legs in midfield
and David's were the only ones available.
John reluctantly agreed to make way for
him, and Graham dropped back deeper to
try and stiffen their resistance for the last
ten minutes.

But they could not stem the tide and
Waverley's striped waves continued to
surge towards Ricky's goal. Through tiredness, Mr Kenning could see alarming gaps

appearing in Sandford's defensive shield, where boys could no longer run to fill them, and his warning shouts were no use.

A simple pass found one of Waverley's strikers with far more space than he would normally have been allowed, and he fired the ball past Ricky without being challenged.

The equalizer came as a terrible blow to Sandford and the defenders looked at each other speechlessly, unable to believe they could have left the Waverley player unmarked right in front of goal.

But worse was to follow. The dam had finally cracked and was now about to burst. Within a minute, a centre from the right had been nodded down by one of the Big 'Uns to Mark on the edge of the area. He crashed the ball up into the roof of the net, clipping the underside of the crossbar on its way in.

'The winner!' he shrieked in excitement. 'That's it!'

Feelings of anguish and exhaustion washed over the Sandford team. Two minutes ago a 2–1 victory had been in their fragile grasp and now they were staring wretchedly at a 2–3 defeat.

Mr Kenning could only sympathize with them. 'One moment you're up and the next you're down in football,' he mused sadly.

How right he was! The game still had one last dramatic sting in its tail.

For perhaps the first time in his young footballing life, even Jeff Thompson felt unable to revive his team, and it took all of Jimmy McDowell's spirited character to gee them up again. He snatched the ball off the dejected Ricky and ran all the way to plonk it on the centre spot for Alan to kick off once more. It seemed like a brave but futile gesture with Waverley so cock-a-hoop and Sandford so demoralized, and less than two minutes remaining on the referee's watch. But Jimmy backed it up with a decisive interception in Waverley's next attack, whipping the ball off the end of the Big 'Un's boot as he was lining up another shot.

The clearance sailed out to Jeff, who summoned up his last reserves of will-power to respond to Jimmy's prompting. He advanced with the ball over the halfway line until a loud, confident call out to his right demanded a pass. Looking across, he transferred it out to David, and the substitute ran free down the flank as Gary moved inside to give him room.

He made good ground past tired oppo-sition, but two more defenders closed down on him to shepherd him over towards the corner flag. Sandford had too many weary legs to get enough players into the box to threaten danger from a centre, and David could see no obvious target. So despite the acute angle, he decided to hit and hope.

The ball curled up high, swung and dipped, and then flew beyond the keeper's straining fingertips into the top far corner of the goal!

'Flighted it perfectly,' was David's answer to his friends' happy cries of 'Fluke!' as they jubilantly half-carried him back to the centre line. They never would believe his claims that it had been more of a deliberate shot than a centre.

Barely had a bewildered Waverley side kicked off again, when Steve blew the final whistle with the score tied at 3–3. Both teams were still in a state of shock at this latest twist of fate, and the players mingled together in relief that their epic contest was all over.

This time Mark did accept Jeff's offer of a handshake in mutual respect.

'I take back everything I've said, we just can't seem to beat you,' Mark admitted with an effort, trying to hide his wounded pride.

Gone now was Mark's arrogant, boastful manner, Jeff noted with satisfaction,

and he too was willing to be on friendlier terms.

'We were lucky to survive near the end,' Jeff conceded, 'but nobody deserved to lose a game like that.'

Mark nodded. 'Jeff,' he said rather bashfully, using his name for the first time, 'sorry about our two new players. They didn't do us much good anyway, but we won't try that sort of thing again.'

They exchanged a smile of understanding.

'That's OK. Just forget it.'

'Thanks, but we shan't forget Sandford in a hurry,' Mark continued. 'We'll stick to playing football like you in future, I think, hard but fair.'

'We'll have to watch out for you then at the next Festival,' Jeff joked and began to turn away towards the hostel.

'There's one more thing I shall never forget as well,' Mark called after him with a laugh.

'Oh, what's that?'

'That tackle of yours!'

10   On the Rocks!

Accompanied by Steve's warning shout, the rope snaked out from the top of the rock face and landed with a thud at Paul's feet some twelve metres below.

He picked up the knotted loop at the end of the safety line and clipped it inside his karabiner, the D-shaped metal attachment dangling from his belt. Mr Kenning checked that Paul screwed up the gate of the karabiner tightly and the rehearsed sequence of climbing calls began.

'Taking in,' Steve informed him from above, hauling in all the slack rope.

'That's me,' Paul responded correctly as it became taut and tugged against him.

'Climb when you're ready,' came the third call.

'Climbing,' Paul shouted but waited, as told, until he heard the fifth and final signal from the instructor.

'OK,' it came, and he cautiously moved on to the rock to start his ascent.

The two instructors had ensured that the boys learned the proper series of calls that climbers use to avoid accidents. They also proved dramatically how the safety line would easily support them if they should slip.

Steve was anchored at the top of the rock face to a stout tree, with the line wound behind his back and over his wrist, while Colin climbed towards him, showing them a possible route up the wall of rock. Suddenly he deliberately toppled backwards into space, to their gasps, but hung suspended as the tight line prevented him from falling.

'If it'll take my weight,' he convinced them, 'it'll certainly take yours. Steve's in charge up there.'

Now Steve gradually took in the surplus rope as Paul clawed his way up, encouraging him where necessary. 'That's good,

don't rush. Look for suitable footholds first, then finger grips.'

Paul discovered, in fact, that this climb was not too difficult and had plenty of places where the toes of his boots could find support. His confidence grew as he neared the top.

'Well done. You climbed like a mountain goat,' Steve greeted him as he clambered over the edge and stood up, panting slightly, but pleased to have accomplished his first ever piece of real rock climbing without mishap.

Monday morning's climbing session had started early after a refreshing, undisturbed night's sleep. It was designed to provide them with new skills and challenging experiences, but before it was through it would test their nerve and courage too.

They began with some gentle clambering around the foot of the cliff and then traversed a narrow, awkward ledge only a metre or so off the ground. They had to pick their way along, one after the other, selecting likely foot and handholds among the chinks and crevices in the limestone rock, and keep their balance until jumping off at the end.

From there they graduated on to the vertical climb and several of the party had already completed it. Paul skirted around the cliff top, well away from the edge, to join them where they were waiting with Mr Turner, while Colin prepared the next stage of their activities. They now faced the daunting prospect of abseiling on a rope, back down a higher, sheer rock face!

Meanwhile, Steve threw the line down again to the remaining helmeted boys below, ready for David's turn to repeat the process of roping up and reciting the ritual calls before climbing.

'I could have done it without a rope easily,' he boasted when he eventually reached the top.

'I'm sure you could,' Steve said. 'You did

all the work then. I wasn't helping by pulling you up. It's only there just in case. Better to be safe than sorry, eh?'

'I guess so,' David shrugged.

'The biggest danger is over-confidence, taking risks, that's when accidents can happen. Check everything – knots, ropes, karabiners, the lot. There's a more difficult climb later on and you might be glad of a rope on that. No fears, no tears! Right?'

David had to agree, but he was already looking across to where the abseiling was under way.

Colin had earlier demonstrated the technique with the ease that only comes with much practice, leaning right back almost horizontally away from the cliff, with just his feet making brief contact as he bounced down the rock on the rope. He reached the bottom in only a matter of seconds.

'Phew! It's a bit like *Spiderman*!' Graham whispered.

He was more concerned than most as

they looked at each other in alarm. They knew they all had to attempt it, but Graham had volunteered to go first as the guinea-pig, an offer about which he was now having second thoughts. After years of being warned to stay away from cliff edges, he was soon going to be asked to step over one backwards!

Colin had rigged up a complex network of support ropes around trees and stakes to make the abseil absolutely safe, but still there were doubts in their faces. Each one harboured nagging fears that if anything did go wrong, it would be bound to happen to him!

Graham found himself strapped into a kind of harness around the tops of his legs, referred to by Colin as his nappy to make him laugh and ease his tension. The harness was connected by karabiners to the abseil rope.

'Hold the rope in front with your left hand but don't grip it too hard,' Colin explained. 'Remember you can control the

speed of your descent by locking and releasing the rope in your right hand. Move it away from your body to let you go down and bring it back across you to brake if you think you're going too fast.'

Graham thought he understood, but the very first stage of the operation was the most nerve-racking of his whole life. Standing on the brink of the cliff with his back to the drop, his feet and legs refused to obey him, they felt so shaky. Finally he had to kneel down before slithering over the edge. He hoped the others would not recognize how scared he was inside, although he was trying hard not to show it.

It would have been so easy to chicken out of it and ask Colin to pull him back up on the safety line, but he resisted the impulse. He gathered all his courage before it could fail him.

The first two metres were the worst. As Graham lost sight of his friends, watching anxiously from behind the instructor, and struggled to plant both his feet on the rock, a choking wave of panic gripped him. But somehow he forced it back down and felt a great surge of relief. He suddenly realized that he did indeed have control of the situation, and that he was not going to crash down on to the rocky floor swaying beneath him.

His fears melted away, and to his surprise he found that he was enjoying it!

'Good lad, you're getting the hang of it,' Colin praised him. 'Try and lean out more, straighten up, and let the rope out nice and smoothly.'

Graham now felt much better and was even confident enough to press harder against the rock with his feet to manage a bit of a spaceman's bounce away from it.

'Wow! Look at Graham,' he heard from below and that gave him a great boost.

'Give them a wave with your left hand, it's perfectly safe to let go,' Colin called. 'Show them there's nothing to worry about.'

He hardly dared to do that, but he did manage a little flutter before clutching the line again. It took him a while to walk backwards down the rest of the cliff and he was quite sorry when his feet touched the ground.

Detaching himself from the various fittings, he waited at the bottom to watch Jimmy's efforts, amazed at his own achievement and knowing what thoughts were racing through his friend's mind.

Jimmy was equally nervous but took encouragement from Graham's survival.

'What's it like?' he shouted.

'Ace!' came back the answer, as Graham basked in the satisfaction of having it behind him, while the others still had to sweat it out before going through the ordeal.

Jimmy shared the same feelings of regret as he passed the point of no return just below the cliff top, but as he learned how to check his progress with his right hand, he breathed more easily. His descent was a little untidy, dangling down vertically for a time when his feet slid off the rock, but he was not too bothered about winning points for personal style!

'Once you've got past that first bit, it's OK, isn't it?' he gabbled upon reaching the ground.

'Sure is,' Graham agreed. 'Hope there's a chance for another go later.'

There was, but only after everybody had fought their private terrors when going 'over the top', as Jeff termed it, and sampled the delights of abseiling for the first time. Then, of course, before

they could relive the experience and try to improve their technique, they had to climb back up again!

The second ascent was more arduous and proved very tricky to everyone bar Scott, who earned the nickname of 'the Monkey' from Dale. The rock was smoother, with fewer obvious holds, and several of them were grateful for the rope support after a slip or when they found themselves rather stuck.

David was one who missed his footing on an insecure crack and was left hanging helplessly at the end of the safety line in Steve's reliable hands.

'Point taken?' the instructor smiled as David regained his position, and the boy nodded, a little pale, an important lesson learned.

Later Steve made them all laugh, and Gary blush, when he told him not to hug the rock as though it was his girlfriend. 'Don't press yourself flat against it or you can't look around for your next hold properly,' he went on.

They tried to imagine anyone at school wanting to be Gary's girlfriend!

Dean Walters was the only one of the group to encounter genuine difficulties. He became stranded on the first climb when his legs turned to jelly, and he suffered badly from the jitters attempting the abseil. Getting more and more upset and angry with himself, he repeatedly tried and failed to overcome his fears about going over the cliff. But he refused to admit defeat and was determined to do it, receiving every encouragement and help from the other boys and teachers alike. They remembered how close they had come themselves to giving in.

Finally, to his credit, he succeeded and was bucked up by their cheers when he landed in a heap at the bottom, trembling with the effort.

'Once is enough,' he tried to joke when offered another chance. 'I think I've found out today I don't like heights!'

Both the teachers had joined in wholeheartedly, hoping not to make a hash of it in front of the children, but they took a lot of teasing during their unsteady abseils as all eyes watched expectantly for the slightest mistake.

By the end of the hectic, strenuous morning some of them felt almost ready to tackle Mount Everest, although they soon proved more eager to tackle their packed lunches.

As they sat around on the valley slopes munching their meal, the talk was all about the new sport and how they had coped, football – at least for a while – not being the major topic of their conversation.

'I reckon I wouldn't mind taking it up when I'm a bit older,' Jeff announced. 'Maybe join a climbing club. Abseiling's fantastic once you get used to it.'

'Well, it is the second quickest way down,' Dale began, setting the trap.

It was Jimmy who plunged in without stopping to think. 'What's the fastest then?'

'Falling!' Dale laughed delightedly, until he choked on his sandwich and Paul bonked him on the top of his protective helmet which he had forgotten to remove.

Mr Kenning interrupted their frivolities. 'Right, glad to hear you all enjoyed it so much. You've been up in the world this morning, and now you're about to find out what it's like to go down into the depths of the Earth . . !'

11 Down into the Depths

Caving! The boys eagerly awaited whatever lay in store for them here. It conjured up exciting possibilities of danger and mystery. They had all read stories about underground adventures.

Not only that, the instructors had promised them that they were going to get extremely wet and filthy! All part of the fun.

After lunch they returned the climbing gear to the hostel's minibuses and exchanged it for the caving equipment, more rope, peaked helmets, lamps and battery packs. The lamps clipped on to the front of their helmets and were attached by leads to the heavy batteries which they wore strapped to their backs.

'Cor! This battery weighs a ton,' puffed Andrew. 'Why can't we just hold a torch, Steve?'

'Because you need your hands free to crawl along in places and to carry things. Here, catch!'

He flung him a large coil of rope and Andrew groaned. It made the trudge up the steep valley to the cave entrance in the afternoon sunshine even warmer work for him!

'Here it is,' Colin announced at last.

'Where?'

'Just up there.'

They still did not make it out immediately. The opening looked impossibly small. Mr Turner assessed his chances of squeezing through the low-roofed gap in the side of the hill and looked doubtful.

Colin laughed, reading his mind. 'This is no cave for the general public with fancy electric lighting. It's a get down and wriggle place!'

'Lead on,' the Headmaster smiled ruefully. 'If you can get through, so will I, somehow.'

'We'll give you a push if you get stuck,' Colin said, only half-jokingly.

They switched on their lamps to test them, and then, one by one, squirmed underneath the shelf of rock. Once inside they found, to their surprise, that they could stand up as the cave widened and increased in height, but they had left the daylight behind. Now only the beams from the lamps lit the darkness, and they looked around them in the eerie half-light cast by twenty illuminated helmets.

'I'll lead the way further in,' Colin said. 'Steve'll bring up the rear, so everybody stay somewhere between us. There are a lot of other tunnels branching off. Most of them are dead ends but we don't want anyone straying and getting lost.'

'Not when we still have one more match to play tomorrow,' Jeff put in, wryly.

They burrowed deeper into the hillside, the floor at times level and then dropping down, occasionally quite steeply, as they followed the channel worn out of the rock by the unrelenting force of an underground river over millions of years. They could hear water somewhere but this section of the tunnel was dry, apart from some muddy patches.

They stumbled and groped their way along, stooping or crawling on their hands and knees where necessary, and even slithering on their stomachs or backs, according to their own preferred style, when the roof came down very low. Head first or feet first, it did not seem to matter as long as they continued to make progress in their strange new surroundings.

The batteries on their backs caused problems until they became more accustomed to their extra bulk, but at least their helmets saved them from some painful scrapes and bangs on the head when they failed to spot some protruding piece of rock.

Colin, at length, called a halt for a breather where the passage opened out, but they had to squat down to be comfortable. Standing upright was now a rare luxury. He told them to switch off their lights and immediately they were plunged into total and absolute pitch-blackness.

'Where's my hand gone?' murmured Paul, knowing it was only a few centimetres from his face, but nothing could be seen.

'Just to show you that you would have no chance of finding your way out of such a cave without the proper equipment,' came Colin's voice, and then without warning there was a flash of light.

A flickering flame of a candle appeared, and his pale features seemed to float in the air behind it.

'Anybody know any good ghost stories?' the face questioned.

'Oh, don't!' pleaded Jimmy's voice. 'Not here, it's too spooky.'

Wwhhhooooooohh!!

The terrible wail was quickly followed by a few stifled shrieks.

'Gary!' Scott cried out, recognizing the joker. 'Don't do that!'

'You idiot, Gary!' David scolded him. 'You nearly scared the wits out of me.'

Gary enjoyed his little triumph but he too was quite glad when all the lamps were flipped back on.

Their earlier abseiling experience was now put to good use, sooner than anticipated, when they discovered that the floor dropped away sharply into the depths. Roped up to their karabiners, they half-scrambled, half-slid down the slope, relying on the line that Steve expertly paid out for support. Even Dean managed the tricky descent quite well, the gloom obscuring the rocky bottom until he was almost standing safely upon it.

'I suppose we've got to climb back up that later,' he sighed.

''Fraid so,' Colin confirmed. 'It's the only way out unless you're wearing diving gear and can swim through the underground stream.'

The wider passage now narrowed once more into an extremely low, wet channel where they had to flatten themselves to the muddy floor and creep through the puddles of dirty water. It was a very tight fit in places and the teachers did indeed worry what might happen if they became stuck! All that could be seen were the scrabbling feet of the person in front.

Everyone was mightily relieved to emerge finally into a broad cavern, where they could actually straighten up again and talk to one another.

'Good job we're wearing old, scruffy clothes today,' Alan laughed. 'Just look at the mess they're in!'

'My mum'll have a fit when she sees mine!' Jimmy exclaimed. 'They'll have to be thrown out, I bet, after this.'

'I never believed we were going to get so mucky,' Scott joined in. 'This is great!'

Before them lay the dark, calm surface of a small subterranean lake.

'We've got to skirt round this,' Colin told them, 'but be careful you don't fall in. There's said to be a monster lurking in it.'

They laughed, but privately did not quite know whether to believe him or not.

'Try to keep out of the water, but there's not much to cling on to along the edge.'

There wasn't. The lake completely covered the cavern floor and the sides were sloping and slippery. Crouched low in the dark to maintain their balance, they pressed themselves against the wall and picked their way slowly and carefully along the uneven rocks. Sometimes they could find extra support by resting one hand on the bumpy ceiling just above their heads.

It was hard work, putting a lot of strain on their legs. The cavern was filled with the noise of their heavy breathing, grunts of effort, scraping of boots and the inevitable splashes when their feet slithered into the shallows, to be followed by a few laughs.

Suddenly there was a bigger and louder splash.

'The monster!' shrieked Sammy.

'No, it's not. It's only Ricky,' Graham shouted. 'He's gone for a swim.'

Ricky had missed his footing altogether and slid helplessly into the pool, up to his knees and elbows in the icy cold water.

He did not bother to climb back out but waded on through the water to the far side,

where the others shortly joined him on dry land. They chortled unsympathetically at his misfortune, many of them having wet feet too.

'Uggh! My jeans are soaked,' he moaned. 'They're all horrible and soggy now.'

'Never mind, Ricky, you'll dry out,' said Steve. 'Let's press on.'

'Where to?'

'You'll see.'

It was worth all the effort. The going was easier now. They had a chance to examine the walls of the tunnel and find good examples of fossil remains of ancient shell creatures embedded in the limestone rock.

Then they turned a corner and their eyes were treated to a spectacular formation of stalactites and stalagmites as their light beams caught the glistening sparkle of drops of water on the limestone deposits.

This was journey's end and they rested a while to admire the slender clusters hanging from the walls and ceilings, and the shorter, stubbier stalagmites jutting up from the floor.

'They've been growing very slowly for an extremely long time, so be careful not to snap any off,' the Headmaster said. 'One second of destruction can ruin thousands of years of creation.'

When they had gazed their fill, Steve broke the bad news about retracing their steps.

'Not round the lake again!' cried Ricky.

'That's right. Do you want a pair of flippers this time?'

They negotiated it with similar difficulty, but no 'monster' splashes this time. They squeezed up the narrow tunnel, and it was only when they were about to climb back up the slope on the rope that Mr Kenning heard a familiar question. It was enough to send a chill tingle up his spine.

'Where's Gary?'

He looked desperately around the dirt-smeared, grubby faces, realizing that he had not seen or heard Gary either for some while.

'This isn't April Fool's Day any more, you know. It's not another prank, is it?'

The serious looks convinced him that this was no laughing matter, not even for them.

His eyes met Mr Turner's and their hearts sank at the thought of what might have happened to Gary.

'How on earth could he have got separated from us?' Mr Kenning demanded. 'Surely if he were lost, he would have shouted.'

They all listened, keeping perfectly still, but there was only a trickle of water to be heard. Neither was there any response to their own calls.

'Gary! Why is it always Gary?' the teacher said aloud in exasperation.

'It doesn't need all of us going back,' Steve decided. 'I know these caves well. Don't worry, we'll find him quickly. As long as he doesn't panic and do something silly, he'll be all right.'

It was swiftly agreed that Colin and the Headmaster should lead the party out while Mr Kenning returned with Steve. As he tried to keep up with the instructor's rapid pace, he was haunted by terrible pictures of the boy's possible fate. He could almost imagine the newspaper headlines of the cave tragedy on Sandford's Tour!

The two men paused and listened in vain.

'I'm beginning to think this was deliberate,' Steve whispered.

'Deliberate? You mean, he meant to give us the slip?'

'I reckon so. What's he like? Would he do that sort of thing?'

'Gary? He's capable of doing anything,'

166

the teacher sighed.

'There's only one place he can be, then.'

'Not the lake?'

'No. The stalactites. Come on!'

Relief flooded over Mr Kenning as they approached the chamber and saw a small light ahead of them. 'You wait here, Steve. I'll go and talk to the boy.'

'I heard you calling and coming back,' Gary greeted him calmly. 'The sounds echo for miles.'

'Then why didn't you answer them?'

'I don't know. I just like it here. I wanted to stay.'

They sat together on a rock for a while in silence, gazing in wonder at the weird shadow effects their lights cast on the walls. The teacher was, for once, lost for words. He had never seen Gary in this peculiar mood, seemingly enchanted by the display of stalactites.

'They're beautiful,' Gary murmured suddenly. 'The shadows make all kinds of

shapes if you look closely, animals' heads and things.'

'You should have said before. We could all have stayed a little longer.'

'It wouldn't have been the same. The others were too noisy. It's best when it's quiet on your own. I just switched off my light until you'd all gone.'

Mr Kenning had to admire the boy's nerve, staying alone in the dark, deep underground. The difficulty of getting out again had not seemed to occur to him. But this was not the time for telling him off for causing them all that unnecessary concern.

'C'mon now, we'd better go back and join the others,' he suggested.

Gary didn't stir.

'I don't think I want to go back, Mr Kenning,' he said and then hesitated. 'I mean, go back home. The Tour's been so great, I just wish it could go on for ever.'

The teacher nodded and began to understand the situation better. He guessed that

Gary would not be going home to much of a welcome, but he hoped that he might be wrong. Staying in the cavern had partly been Gary's way of expressing his mixed-up feelings.

'Well, the Tour's not over yet. We've got one more game left, remember. But we've all got to go home some time.'

'I suppose so,' Gary sighed and stood up, and then looked very worried. 'What will you tell the others? They'll think I'm even more stupid if they find out I was just sitting on my own down here.'

'No, they won't,' Mr Kenning reassured him, leading him back up the passage. 'We'll tell them you liked caving so much you went off to explore some more tunnels by yourself. How about that? They'll be green with envy.'

Gary grinned. 'But I really *do* like it. I'm gonna be a caver when I'm older. I've decided!'

But after struggling up through all the

twisting tunnels again, they were both pleased to blink their way back out into the bright sunlight at the cave mouth, emerging head first to the relieved cheers of the rest of the anxious group.

Gary was quickly swallowed up by them and became the centre of attention. He would now have a real tale of his own to tell about his underground adventures!

12 Homeward Bound

'Is the coach here yet?' Jeff asked as Scott popped back into their now almost bare dormitory.

'No. Just checking I hadn't left anything.'

'So were we,' said Graham, not caring to admit their reluctance to leave the hostel for the final time. 'Found some sweets down the side of the bunk from last night's feast.'

'Feast!' exclaimed Jeff. 'I'd hardly call a few sweets and biscuits a feast.'

'No, well, it was the best we could do,' he shrugged.

'Dale said they had a cake in their room,' Scott put in.

Graham snorted. 'Don't believe him, he'll say anything to make you jealous.'

'They were making enough noise, anyway,' Jeff added. 'I don't know what time we all got to sleep.'

'We had to make the most of the last night, didn't we?' Scott sighed. 'We've sure had some fun here.'

'Yep, but it's time to go, I guess,' Jeff stated. 'Let's go and say cheerio to Steve and Colin, and then see what's keeping that coach. I want to get stuck into Lynfield!'

The Tour party had passed a leisurely morning packing up their belongings, tidying rooms and doing some souvenir hunting in town. Their pocket money was now all spent on small presents like badges, key rings and pens to take back home.

There had even been time for a light-hearted kickabout on the recreation ground, during which Mark and some of the Waverley team showed up. They accepted Jeff's friendly invitation to join in.

Mark, though smiling, couldn't resist a parting shot. 'You'll have to come again some time and we'll give you a beating then instead!'

172

'Perhaps we will,' Jeff laughed. 'But get some practice in – you'll need it!'

Their picnic lunch was interrupted first by the arrival of the coach and then by the only rain on the Tour, and they had to finish it off inside its steamed-up windows.

'April showers!' the driver forecast. 'It'll clear up soon before your match. Here, I've got a copy of the *Frisborough Journal* for you to look at.'

The newspaper was passed around and read with great interest. The back page carried a report of their Festival success with everyone's name mentioned!

The instructors waved the boys off on their homeward journey, and the footballers' thoughts concentrated more on the approaching fixture with Lynfield Junior School. Lynfield's sports master, Mr Wainwright, had told his players to report back to school from their Easter holidays for the two o'clock kick-off against the tourists.

As they neared their destination, it dawned on those in Year Six that this was something of a farewell performance in Sandford's all-red strip.

'I can hardly believe this is our last game together,' Jeff began. 'We've got to finish in style and go out with a big win. Spread it round the coach . . . we're looking for goals!'

Mr Kenning had promised everybody a game at some point today, but had not yet announced the starting line-up. Whatever plans he did have, however, were soon altered when they reached Lynfield and Mr Wainwright explained his problems.

'I'm afraid one of our crossbars has been smashed by some hooligans over the weekend. We've got witnesses, though, and I'm calling in the local police later. They're not going to get away with causing such stupid damage.'

'The vandals!' Mr Kenning replied, shaking his head. 'It doesn't make any sense, does it?'

'In the meantime, as you can see, I've strung some rope tightly across the top of the posts as a rough guide. It's not satisfactory but it's the same for both sides. The other matter is even more embarrassing.'

'What's that?'

'We're a player short, unfortunately. One of our attackers has gone off on holiday, and I'm told my reserve is ill and won't be turning up. We only have ten men. I wondered if we might borrow one of yours?'

'Of course,' Mr Kenning agreed, and then was struck by a sudden idea and chuckled. 'In fact I think I've got just the man for the job. It won't bother him at all to play against his own team. I think you'll like him . . .'

So it was that Gary, now highly regarded as a fearless caver, trotted out on to the pitch wearing a yellow Lynfield shirt, grinning like a Cheshire cat at all the teasing.

'Sandford's new record transfer,' Dale

called out gleefully. 'One million pounds and a bag of sweets for Gary Clarke, Super-sub and Penalty King!'

But behind the joking, there was some concern in the camp. They suspected that Gary might be out to prove a point or two at their expense. If he were on song, he spelled trouble for any defence.

Mr Kenning made sure they paid attention to marking him closely, and also that they loosened up properly before the kick-off after their experience at Bradbury.

'Good luck,' he said to them. 'Just go out and do your stuff.'

With four substitutes standing by, they lined up in their usual 4–3–3 formation:

Robin

Jimmy Scott Andrew Paul

John Jeff Graham

David Alan Dale

The rain cleared away for the duration of the game, but the wetness of the grass helped Sandford to make an ideal start, quite the opposite to their opening Tour game.

After only four minutes play, a drive from Jeff skidded off the greasy surface, the extra pace and low bounce deceiving the goalkeeper who was unable to hold on to the ball. Alan, who had followed up the shot as every good striker should, had no difficulty in turning it over the line to put them one goal ahead.

'That's the first,' Jeff shouted. 'No letting up. We want more.'

Lynfield may have started the game in a more relaxed, holiday mood than the touring team, but as the local cup-winners themselves, they had no wish to be regarded as push-overs. They realized they had a full blooded game on their hands – the visitors obviously meant business!

At first the home side treated Gary cautiously, believing that they had probably been landed with a duffer. But they soon saw he could play a bit when he pushed the ball cheekily through Paul's legs and brought a good save out of the goalkeeper. Their confidence in him grew.

Robin impressed again shortly afterwards, when he dived low to his left to get his body well behind the line of the ball in case it eluded his gloved hands. Mr Kenning took comfort from the knowledge that Sandford's goal would be in safe keeping for another two years at least.

But Sandford were in no mood to defend for long, and struck again with a classic headed goal.

David took an inswinging corner from the left, curling it into the goalmouth with his right foot. Graham rose to meet it perfectly at the near post and glanced it accurately and skilfully into the far corner of the net.

They nearly made it three as well when first a shot from David himself clipped the foot of a post, and then later Alan put one into the side netting. So it came as even more of a stunning blow when, just before half-time, Lynfield pulled a goal back and dented their hopes of a crushing victory.

It was a cruel piece of luck for Robin, as he appeared to have the shot well covered until it took a sharp deflection off another forward and spun away into the opposite side of the goal to which he had dived.

With the interval score at 2–1, things had not exactly gone according to plan, but they

remained optimistic. At least they had kept Gary reasonably quiet so far. The teachers sorted out the substitutions in defence, restoring Ricky in goal and replacing Andrew and Jimmy with Ian and Sammy. Dean still looked rather pale and they decided not to use him until the final few minutes. He had woken up complaining of a stomach ache, but Mr Kenning considered it to be more the lingering effects of the previous day's upsets on the rocks and perhaps a touch of homesickness.

The second half began in topsy-turvy fashion. Sandford thought they had gone 3-1 ahead when a defence-splitting pass from John sent Alan clear to steer the ball expertly home. He turned round in dismay to see the referee signalling for offside, having failed to hear the whistle.

'Only just,' Mr Wainwright explained, 'but when the ball was kicked, you were standing in an offside position.'

Alan accepted the decision without any fuss. He had wondered why the keeper hadn't dived for his shot!

Instead of enjoying a comfortable lead, the scores were quickly levelled at 2–2. And to make matters worse, the equalizer came from the striker on loan!

Gary's ability to kill a ball with one silky touch gave him the time and space he needed to select his spot and leave Ricky helpless with a well-placed shot.

His new team-mates were delighted, but not half as much as Gary, whose broad, smug grin infuriated Sandford.

'Whose side is he on, anyway?' Scott grumbled bitterly. 'He's sabotaging our plans.'

'We've thrown away a two-goal lead,' Jeff said, in disgust. 'We're not going to lose our last game, whatever Gary may think.'

Gary did not really care what the final result might be. The way he looked at it, he wouldn't lose whatever happened.

Sandford piled on more pressure, but their frustrations were summed up when a clever dipping shot from Dale twanged the rope and flopped harmlessly over.

'Just my luck!' he cried. 'If that had been a proper crossbar, it would probably have gone in off the underside.'

'I thought we'd seen enough ropes yesterday,' Paul called out, in annoyance.

Scott, though, brought a smile back to their faces. 'It'll come in useful later. We'll hang Gary from the other crossbar with it!'

The remark, however, certainly made Gary keep out of Scott's way for a while.

But eventually the vital breakthrough came, as Graham coolly slotted home his second goal after a neat exchange of passes with Dale. Theirs was a deadly combination which had provided many goals for both of them over the season.

'They won't catch us again now,' Jeff predicted.

It was Jeff himself who made certain that was correct. David's sprinting speed took him to the by-line and he screwed the ball diagonally backwards for the captain to hit it in his stride. It whistled through the net-less goal and clattered into the fence behind before anyone could make a move for it.

Inspired by Jeff's dynamic example, Sandford gained complete mastery over the opposition and scored two further

goals. Firstly Graham celebrated a fine hat-trick with a fierce volley, to cap an excellent personal Tour for him after his winning goal in the Sevens.

Then, as Dean appeared for a run on the wing to replace Dale, Sammy King opened his goal account for the school in the same match that Jeff had scored his last. It was an unforgettable, thrilling moment for him.

Sammy stayed up for a corner after supporting an attack, and to his amazement, as he stood unmarked on the edge of the area, the ball was half cleared towards him. It bobbled up invitingly as he took careful aim, and he fired it clean through a crowded goalmouth and low inside a post.

That made the score 6–2, but the Tour was not over yet. It ended in an incident of high drama in a most unusual and bizarre manner.

With just two minutes left, Ian tried to control an awkward bouncing ball in front of goal and was seen to handle it.

Although it was accidental, his opponent had been prevented from shooting and the referee was obliged to award a penalty.

Before anyone could react, Lynfield's new player picked up the ball and marched with it to the penalty spot. Only then did people realize what Gary intended to do and the protests began.

'He can't take it, he'll miss on purpose.'

'I doubt that, judging by the way he's performed so far,' Mr Wainwright said, but he was still uncertain how serious the boy was. Like everybody else, he had never come across such a situation before.

But when the distressed Sandford goalkeeper also joined in the protests, muttering about it being unfair, Lynfield changed their minds.

'OK, let him take it,' the home captain agreed. 'It doesn't really matter now whether he scores or not. It should be good for a laugh.'

But it was no laughing matter for poor

Ricky! He settled on the line, tensed and re-signed to his fate, while everyone watched in total fascination.

Gary confidently and deliberately placed the ball, enjoying himself hugely. 'Which way is it going, Ricky?' he teased.

The colour drained from Ricky's face. 'Just shut up and get on with it,' he answered tersely.

Gary decided to stick it to Ricky's left and skipped in with a little shimmy of his body. Ricky had had many chances recently to study Gary's penalty technique and ig-nored his dummy wiggle. He had already made up his mind to dive to his left!

Somehow he got across to the spot-kick and blocked it with his arms.

'He's missed it!' went up the cry and it jolted Gary out of his shock. He pounced on the loose ball before Ricky could smother it and poked it over the line.

The two gladiators collapsed to the ground together in different states of agony and ecstasy, before being hauled to their feet by willing hands to console and congratulate.

'Brilliant, Ricky!' Jeff cried. 'A blinding save. Duncan wouldn't have smelt it.'

Gary, too, patted him on the back and Ricky managed a smile. 'Oh well, at least

I stopped the first one. There aren't many keepers who can say that!'

The game ended almost immediately, 6–3 in favour of Sandford, who could claim to have scored eight of the goals, and the two teams cheered each other off the field.

'Some team you've got there,' Mr Wainwright assessed. 'There's no stopping them. It can't be bad if you can afford to lend us someone like that Gary.'

'You said it,' Mr Kenning replied contentedly, 'but we almost regretted it. What a marvellous way to finish!'

It had indeed been a spectacular victory, and Gary was quickly forgiven as they ragged each other unmercifully on the journey home, everyone in high spirits.

They were looking forward to seeing familiar faces and places again after nearly a week away from home.

'I've missed my dog,' Paul said, and then added to hoots of laughter, 'but not my little sister!'

'Well, that's that. Tour's over, I guess,' sighed Jeff sadly. 'Athletics and cricket next term, though. Have to get cracking with some training. Got to keep fit.'

'Fit!' exclaimed Dale, slumped deep down into the back seat. 'Fit to drop, you mean.

All I want to do now is to crawl into my own little bed and catch up on some sleep.'

But there was certainly no chance of anyone dozing on the coach. It was a noisy, happy trip back to Sandford, with joking and singing all the way.

Like Dale, they were going to need the rest of the Easter holidays to recover from being on Tour!

THE END

Appendix

Tour Results and Goal Scorers
Football Festival
'A' Team Group

West Norton 0 – 2 Sandford 'A' (Dale 2)
Havendon 4 – 1 Market Peyton 'B'
Havendon 1 – 1 Sandford 'A' (Graham)
West Norton 3 – 1 Market Peyton 'B'
Market Peyton 'B' 0 – 1 Sandford 'A' (David)
West Norton 1 – 1 Havendon

	P	W	D	L	F	A	Pts
Sandford 'A'	3	2	1	0	4	1	5
Havendon	3	1	2	0	6	3	4
West Norton	3	1	1	1	4	4	3
Market Peyton 'B'	3	0	0	3	2	8	0

'B' Team Group

Bridgeford 2 – 2 Sandford 'B' (John, Alan)
Tanby 1 – 0 Church Fentley
Church Fentley 2 – 1 Sandford 'B' (Alan)
Tanby 3 – 0 Bridgeford
Church Fentley 3 – 1 Bridgeford
Tanby 1 – 1 Sandford 'B' (Dean)

	P	W	D	L	F	A	Pts
Tanby	3	2	1	0	5	1	5
Church Fentley	3	2	0	1	5	3	4
Sandford 'B'	3	0	2	1	4	5	2
Bridgeford	3	0	1	2	3	8	1

Semi-Finals

Dartingham 1 – 3 Sandford 'A' (Graham,
Scott, Gary)

Waverley 'A' 3 – 2 Tanby

Final

Waverley 'A' 1 – 2 Sandford 'A' (Jeff,
Graham)

Friendly Matches

Bradbury 2 – 1 Sandford (Alan)

Waverley 3 – 3 Sandford (Dale, Gary,
pen., David)

Lynfield 3 – 6 Sandford (Graham 3,
Alan, Jeff, Sammy)
(Gary 2, for Lynfield)

FOR SPORTS FANS EVERYWHERE!

A SELECTED LIST OF TITLES AVAILABLE FROM YOUNG CORGI YEARLING BOOKS, ALSO BY ROB CHILDS

THE PRICES SHOWN BELOW WERE CORRECT AT THE TIME OF GOING TO PRESS. HOWEVER TRANSWORLD PUBLISHERS RESERVE THE RIGHT TO SHOW NEW RETAIL PRICES ON COVERS WHICH MAY DIFFER FROM THOSE PREVIOUSLY ADVERTISED IN THE TEXT OR ELSEWHERE.

☐	0 552 52824 2	**THE BIG CHANCE**	£2.99
☐	0 552 52581 2	**THE BIG DAY**	£3.50
☐	0 552 54297 0	**THE BIG FOOTBALL COLLECTION OMNIBUS***	£4.99
☐	0 552 52804 8	**THE BIG GAME**	£2.99
☐	0 552 52760 2	**THE BIG GOAL**	£2.50
☐	0 552 52663 0	**THE BIG KICK**	£3.50
☐	0 552 52451 4	**THE BIG MATCH**	£2.99
☐	0 552 52823 4	**THE BIG PRIZE**	£2.99
☐	0 552 52825 0	**THE BIG STAR**	£2.99
☐	0 440 86318 X	**SOCCER AT SANDFORD**	£2.99
☐	0 440 86320 1	**SANDFORD ON TOUR**	£2.99
☐	0 440 86350 3	**ALL GOALIES ARE CRAZY**	£2.99
☐	0 440 86344 9	**SOCCER MAD**	£2.99

* contains The Big Game, The Big Match and The Big Prize

All Transworld titles are available by post from:

Book Service By Post, P.O. Box 29, Douglas, Isle of Man IM99 1BQ

Credit cards accepted. Please telephone 01624 675137,
fax 01624 670923, Internet http://www.bookpost.co.uk or
e-mail: bookshop@enterprise.net for details.

Free postage and packing in the UK. Overseas customers allow
£1 per book (paperbacks) and £3 per book (hardbacks).

SOCCER AT SANDFORD

ROB CHILDS

'We're going to have a fantastic season!'

Jeff Thompson is delighted to be picked as captain of Sandford Primary School's football team. With an enthusiastic new teacher and a team full of talent – not least that of loner Gary Clarke, with his flashes of goal-scoring brilliance – he is determined to lead Sandford to success. Their goal is the important League Championship – and their main rivals are Tanby, who they must first meet in a vital Cup-tie . . .

From kick-off to the final whistle, through success and disappointment, penalties and corners, to the final nail-biting matches of the season, follow the action and the excitement as the young footballers of Sandford Primary School learn how to develop their skills and mould together as a real team – a team who are determined to win by playing the best football possible!

0 440 86318 X